CN0069125I

ESSEX
GHOST
TALES

ESSEX GHOST TALES

ROBERT HALLMANN

ILLUSTRATED BY CLAIRE BARTLETT

The History Press

For Minna and Theo

First published 2015

The History Press
The Mill, Brimscombe Port
Stroud, Gloucestershire, GL5 2QG
www.thehistorypress.co.uk

British Library Cataloguing in Publication Data.
A catalogue record for this book is available from the British Library.

ISBN 978 0 7509 6211 7

Typesetting and origination by The History Press
Printed in Great Britain

CONTENTS

THE SILENT FLEET

When night falls on the ancient coast
And stars abound, the sparkling host
Reflect in ev'ry ripple small,
The night owl hoots its eerie call
            And quietness cloaks all,

Then rises proud a silent fleet
Of spectres from the muddy deep.
And all the ships that ever sunk
Or rotted on a muddy bank
            Reclaim their naval rank

As ghostly shadows. Floating free,
The lichen hulks take to the sea.
And masts appear where pennents flew.
From Davy's Locker climbs the crew
            And sails unfurl anew.

And black, barge black, the spritsails glide
From friendly quays on wind and tide,
From busy Harwich to the Nore,
From all around the sleeping shore
            Collects the silent corps.

But none who sleep will ever see
The little ships take to the sea
And travel to a foreign strand
To pluck the soldiers from the sand
            As brothers, hand in hand …

Robert Hallmann

INTRODUCTION

The shadows of millennia haunt this land. History is everywhere. There are secrets, sometimes horrible, in families or in the landscape, buried only to escape and take their revenge. All around the convoluting estuary, on the bleak marshes, the sea rises and falls and sometimes releases the dead of centuries from its greedy deep.

Beware the hour of the owl. Avert your eyes when the Gentlemen – gun-packing smugglers – land their stash in some lonely rill close to a forgotten barn or an abandoned vessel, or right under the noses of the Revenue Men. Is that a smuggler or the law that rides quietly through the landscape, heard but not seen? Or something more sinister?

Out on the marshes, wildfowlers glide soundlessly through the reeds or among the tussocks on slim flat boats, waiting for first light, knowledgeable of nature and the habits of its creatures, nine-foot guns pointing out over the rims.

Abroad on the wild heath, old crimes can stay hidden for centuries where shadows abound. Beware the gnarled hanging tree on Gallows Corner. Stay the attention of the highwayman and the footpad when the moon is hiding and the ground is soft. We think we are too wise and enlightened to believe in the old stories, but are you prepared to face your fear out there alone? Moonlight shadows can be deceiving.

Close your ears to the footsteps behind you in the mist, they may well be in your mind. The noises that echo through the old

hall at night, the chilling sounds without a human presence and the flickering light swaying down the deep lane are best ignored, preferably avoided.

Enter the primeval forest that once covered most of Essex. If your conscience is clear you'll have little to fear. Then enter the once-sacred grove and discover its awful secrets. Storms uproot trees. Saxon fights Celt. Old habits die hard. Old gods are reluctant to leave.

When the peripatetic missionaries stepped from their primitive ships and preached their new religion, did the old gods of the Saxons simply roll over and vanish? Was the message of love and forgiveness quietly accepted by men who were looking forward to an eternity of fighting and drinking, served by high-breasted maidens in the mead halls of Valhalla? Would they not have fought, at least in the minds of their followers? Would they have accepted their Götterdämmerung without a struggle?

All their blood and hate soaked into the earth at the sites of the ancient battlefields; would they not demand their remembrance?

The shadows of millennia haunt this land. History is everywhere.

Robert Hallmann, 2015

All illustrations by Claire Bartlett: www.sitandfidget.weebly.com

1

SILENCE OF
THE WOODS

It wasn't the first time he had seen or been approached by someone who wasn't there.

The stranger raised his arm and pointed directly at his heart. 'You think you've got away with it. But I know. You might as well confess now, if you want me to save you.'

Silas Gregson was about to give a defensive answer, or an evasive one, but he could not help his hand feeling for the woodman's knife he carried in his belt. Facing the hooded and shadowy figure, he realised, moments later, that there was no one. Had he imagined it? Was it a figure of his imagination? The trees about him stood silent and majestic as always, though they were old and broad enough to hide someone, should they want to conceal themselves. There were many trees in this large primeval forest.

'Where are you? Who are you? Come out and show yourself!'

He waited, crouching, knife in hand. Where could the owner of that voice be hiding? Silas listened.

Silence.

Nothing but silence. Unnatural silence, it suddenly occurred to him. There was not even birdsong. He shivered. What had he to worry about? He was made of sterner stuff. No one knew, he had convinced himself of that long ago. No one knew and the night had been dark and dismal. No one had ever suspected him, at least not to his face. Until now. Just lately there had been

other occasions. Someone was mocking him. Accusing him. Terrorising him.

Yet there was no one – no one human anyway. Just the old gnarled and misshapen tree nearest to him, twisted and distorted into what might be a grimace, a menacing, gurning grin. An accusing presence.

'It's only a tree, damn it, only a tree …' It was always near trees that he had these pangs of anxiety.

Silas relaxed his coiled stance. He had been on high alert, ready to pounce on whoever had spoken to him in such an accusing tone, but as time passed and nothing happened, he straightened up and calmed down. He had to get a grip. The way he had reacted could have been interpreted as guilt. He should watch his step and act normal.

'It's only a tree,' he repeated under his breath.

As the shock receded he realised the silence was natural again. A woodpigeon cooed and a cuckoo called some distance away. There was even the ak-ak-ak of a woodpecker. It occurred to him that he had not actually seen the owner of the voice. Not actually. He must have imagined it. The stranger had just been a shadow. Anyway, no one could possibly know …

'I know.'

Silas froze again, but only for a moment. He shook his head as if to shake out some bad dream. That voice had come from within. From his heart? His conscience? He thought he had dealt with that. It had to be done and it was for the best. He had convinced himself often enough. Though the world might see it differently, he himself knew it was the only way. It wasn't his fault and that was an end to it. Or so he thought. As he once more looked about him it seemed as if some of the older gnarled and deformed trees were looking at him, pulling faces.

Silas was beginning to hate the woods. He had been surrounded by forest all his life – someone in the past had cleared a fine bit of land that he had inherited – but now he saw shadows behind every tree. Faces grinned at him. Faces like awful distorted masks of hideous creatures taunted him. Every damn tree seemed to be alive and knowing. Whenever possible, he tried to avoid the woods, but it just wasn't always possible.

Without thinking he drove his knife into the scarred bark of the nearest tree, just a little ways, then he jumped back, took a deep breath and scolded himself for being so irrational.

If that had been a human the knife would have penetrated deep.

'You're late,' his wife scolded him. 'Your supper is getting cold. Do you want it warmed up again?'

Silas mumbled about being held up by something, and sat down to his lukewarm plate of rabbit and turnip stew.

His private world of nightmares wouldn't leave him be. Was it Arthur's ghost? He …? It didn't look like Arthur. What or whoever they were was about his own height. Arthur had been a tall fellow, tall and strong. That's why people accepted that he had been wanted by the pressmen. Besides, Arthur wouldn't be the type to haunt him. He was too gentle and good-natured. That's why Margaret had adored him. But why then was it that he was having these visions more and more often as time went by?

'I could kill him …' William, their second son, came in, shook with the cold, threw off his heavy jacket on a chair and walked to the fireplace, slapping his arms about him to encourage the blood flow to his numb fingers. Then he stretched out his hands towards the lusty flickering flames. 'I could …' He grumbled the words as from deep within his being.

'Don't speak like that!' said his mother with concern in her voice. 'Not in this house.'

Only a dismissive growl came from the direction of the fire.

'Who could you kill?' his father asked with as normal a voice as possible.

'That damn brother of mine. He always knows better. Every idea I have he is against. And because he's the elder he always gets his way. It's alright Will, Arthur knows what he is doing …' Raising the pitch of his voice with that last comment, he attempted to imitate his mother's voice.

His father tried to be reasonable. 'Calm down son, that's no way to react to your mother. What's the trouble now? I wish you two would get on and work as a team. You've only got one brother.'

'That's one too many …' As with a sudden decision the young man turned, grabbed his damp coat and made for the door.

'I'm warming up your supper, here …' His mother bustled about, refilling his plate and placing it on the table.

'Keep it for Big Brother. I'm going down to the inn.'

With that he brushed past his mother, threw open the door and slammed it behind him. As his steps receded, the room was left in utter silence for long moments. Now the scraping of Silas Gregson's spoon over the simple tin plate sounded exaggerated in the stillness and the fire suddenly seemed to crackle louder.

It felt like an eternity before Margaret Gregson picked up the courage and broke the silence: 'It's history repeating itself,' she said with ice in her voice. 'It's you and your brother all over again. If Arthur had not been taken by the pressgang, you two would have killed each other.'

Her husband had sat still on the same spot, his head held between his hands. Now he raised his head with a strange look in his eyes, a look she had not seen before. It almost silenced her. Almost. Instead it gave her courage.

'It is true, that he was taken, is it? Strange he has never returned in all this time … nor a sign of life …' She had never before dared to speak her innermost thoughts and doubts. For five long years she had held out, resisting Silas Gregson's advances after Arthur's disappearance, waiting for his return. Eventually she had relented when her brother married and she had fears of remaining alone.

Now her husband jumped up as if stung. His chair toppled backwards and the veins on his temples stood out like ropes.

'My brother is dead … gone.' He corrected himself. 'What are you saying, woman? Are you accusing me? Come on, spit it out! What have you been thinking in that small mind of yours?' His hand was stretched out towards her, palm upwards, his fingers curled inward as if he beckoned her to come nearer. 'Come on, spit it out. You think I had anything to do with it?'

She had never seen her husband so wild. Cowed, she stayed silent. She had always told herself that she was wrong, that her instinct was sinful, as were her thoughts. Now, with her husband's surprise reaction taking her aback, she was not so sure. What if …?

There was no more time to think, as her husband clasped his chest and started coughing in spasms that had her by his side instantly, catching him as he collapsed. She just managing to half guide and half lift him over to the rocking chair by the fire, still coughing and spluttering.

'You shouldn't arouse yourself so. I'm going to make you a poultice …'

'You … try to kill me …? Will you?' The heavily breathing man spat out the words between shaking bouts. In his mind's eye he still saw the girl he'd desired above anything, though nowadays his brother always came between them. 'Whatever did I see in you?' he coughed. 'I should have … left you … to Arthur …'

By the time their eldest son returned for his meal his father had retired to his bed upstairs. His mother began to ladle out the simple fare.

'You're late …'

'I had to bring in the pigs from the woods. Not easy when it's almost dark.'

'Why didn't William help you?'

'He stormed off again. Something upset him. He seems to find nothing to his liking these days. Keeps saying he'll go away to sea like Uncle Arthur. But where is he? And where's Father?' It was more a comment than a question.

His mother looked at him with concern. Deep, deep inside old feelings stirred, feelings of regret, then as quickly faded – he so resembled her missing uncle. Sometimes she thought he was her Arthur of long ago.

'Father's retired. It's his chest again. Those coughing fits will be the death of him if he's not careful. Something is eating away at him. Sometimes I don't hardly recognise him anymore …' She wiped her face with her pinafore to avoid showing her tears.

'And now you and William, fighting just like your father and your uncle used to … Always fighting … What's it this time?'

Arthur had emptied his plate, pushing it away towards his mother. 'Thanks. Tasty rabbit, that.'

'Do you want some more?' she asked. 'There is leftover. Your brother … Your brother didn't stop to eat …' She turned to him with a pot in one hand and a filled ladle in the other.

'Well, if it's going to waste?' Arthur accepted the extra meal with good grace. 'Thanks, Mother … Hope you have eaten yourself.'

With a sudden decision his mother turned back to him, 'Be careful, Arthur, your brother … I'm worried. Your uncle has been away an awful long time and never a word …' She bit her lip as soon as the words had slipped out, regretting her outburst.

Arthur stood up, gripped her upper arms with some concern and looked down intensely into her eyes. 'Mother, what are you saying? You're not suggesting that Father's …? That …? Mother … Is that what you're thinking? Mother …'

She inhaled deeply and placed one hand across her mouth as if to stifle her own voice. 'Forgive me. Please. Forget I ever said it. Please, don't mention it …' She glanced upwards to where her husband was lying abed.

'I heard nothing,' Arthur said confidently, 'and don't you worry. William is wild and he's got his own mind on many things, but he is my brother and he'll calm down. Is Father ill then?'

'He worries me. It's more than just his chest and his coughing. Something's on his mind, something dark.' Then she added on a more practical note: 'What was it this time, you and your brother, I mean?'

'Oh, you know William. He wants to straighten out the track to Burnt Wood hamlet to make the drive straighter and shorter … directly down through the dell and up the steep embankment on the other end. I told him again it'll be the devil's own job. But would he listen to reason? It's too soft in the dell. It'll be murder for the horses that way and just for saving a few minutes' time.'

The atmosphere was charged in the household after that evening. A few uneasy days later and the argument came to a head.

'For once I'll make a decision,' young William shouted. 'The road will be shorter, passing through the dell … Any road, it's of no use. The brush will have to go. It's in the way. It's mostly beech scrub now anyway, apart from the old stumps that are no good to man or beast. It's not even much use for fuel this winter. That oak tree will be useful, though. A beam for the new stable, the one Uncle Arthur started. It's about time that was actually built ... Nice and straight and small enough to be pulled out, roots and all ...' William took the team of horses. 'Won't be a problem.'

The headstrong son ignored his father, defying his word. Arthur tried to talk sense to him, but that only added to his brother's determination. It had become a battle of wills. Who was going to inherit the farm? It seemed that unspoken question was underlying their arguments. William tried to prove himself the more capable, the more worthy, but all he did was antagonise. The quiet Arthur was no match for his cunning, nor his stubborn will. Now the old man followed him to the woods, carrying an axe. Wearily Arthur followed, while Margaret anxiously called after their diminishing figures from the croft doorway, crying and wringing her hands, not knowing what to do.

'Stop them, Arthur, stop them. No, don't you go as well! Oh, please God, someone stop them ...' Torn between the love for her boys and regard for her husband, she collapsed in prayer.

Silas Gregson's chest hurt. Again and again he looked over his shoulder. He was convinced someone was following him. He summoned superhuman strength to overtake William and the horses via a shortcut and there he stopped to listen.

'Remember ... I know ...' said the voice that would be the death of him. But he made it. Behind him Arthur had trouble keeping up.

'You will not!' His father almost shouted the words, now remarkably calm. He moved between William and the thicket. 'That's an ancient site. That was sacred long before Christianity: the sacred grove of the Ancients. It's where the Elders met when the moon was right and when judgements had to be given ...' His voice was slow, low and breathless, but determined. 'Don't raise the ghosts of the past ...'

'What rubbish. You don't believe in that old nonsense, do you? It's a load of scrub and it's in the way. I'll start with that oak. That's what ... maybe twenty-five or thirty years old? Not so ancient, is it? As for the old trunks ...'

'They're ancient oaks. They'll not be touched. They've been here a thousand years …' He started coughing again, now spitting blood, but still he tried to stop his son: 'I'll not have them touched. Do you hear? I'll not have them touched!' In his excitement he began to shake and cough again and he collapsed forward on to the soft forest floor.

The son ignored his father, but now Arthur stepped in, picking up the axe. 'That's enough. Don't you see what it means to the old man? You'd have him dead next. I'll take him back and I need the horses. So leave it be.' With that, Arthur took the reins out of his brother's hand and fastened the dray to the horses' chains. Then he lifted his convulsing father gently on to the simple conveyance, placing the axe by his side.

William stood by, silently, not daring to interfere, but not happy either. Inwardly he was seething. He'd bide his time.

With rest and the doctor's attention, Silas' health had settled down again by the day they went to market. A couple of well-fattened pigs bobbed about and squealed on the small two-wheeled cart as if they had an inkling of the fate that soon would befall them. A wind had come up and at the front on the hard bench seat rode the father and his second son, while his eldest son Arthur walked in front, leading the single horse.

Only their mother was left behind to look after the farm in the woods, but all three men had promised to remember her at the fair. It had been a struggle. She had tried to keep her husband at home to make him rest, yet he was determined not to miss the trading and the gossip. There was no stopping him. At last she suspected he meant to keep an eye on their sons. She had relented, but it had not eased her mind.

A gust of wind gripped the hats of the two men riding the high seat and scattered them back along the track behind them like so many leaves when the small group reached a bend in the road, where gnarled old willows leant over a small stream. Lopping had given the contorted old trunks a top-heavy look from which the new wood rose like unkempt hair from mangled heads, now struggling and bending and flailing in the wind.

With a little imagination one could recognise faces, grimaces, deformed features in the overgrowing bark, but it was not imagination that stirred the father. He had been uneasy as they approached the willows. Now he suddenly rose as in pain and raising his fists to the sky, screaming, he yelled, 'Stop it. It wasn't my fault. Leave me alone …' Then he crumpled back on his stark seat, covering his ears with his fists, just staring ahead of him.

Arthur had halted the horse and rushed after the hats disappearing among a whorl of autumn leaves, retrieving them only slightly the worse for wear. He returned just to see his father's wild gesticulations. Wondering what drove him, he enquired if there was anything that needed to be done.

Next to the old man on the high seat William sat almost unconcerned, his mouth slightly open. He looked at Arthur, then again at his father and back to his brother before shrugging his shoulders and intimating that his father's brains were scrambled.

'Are you all right, Father?' asked Arthur, at the same time listening out for anything untoward in the trees. Only the wind could be heard. What was it his father had reacted to? 'Do you want to turn back?'

It was as if the old man woke at that and he shouted back at his son, 'What are you stopping for? We must get away from here … Go! Go!'

Arthur thought it best to obey and with a tug on the bridle he commanded the horse to move forward, at a faster pace than before. His father sunk back into himself, brooding and muttering and shaking his pale frame.

Most people were familiar in the small community and the brothers joined in the banter with friends and acquaintances. This time it was Silas who made straight for the inn 'to rest his bones' as he put it, trusting his sons with the commercial part of the visit. The inn was crowded and it was only when he began coughing and spluttering that someone made way and allowed him a seat on one of the benches.

'My, does your eldest look like 'is Uncle Arthur. There was a lovely fellow. Thought I'd been asleep and come back to earth thirty years on when I saw 'im … An' he's jus' as polite. Could a had me, could your Arthur, but he were far too polite to ask …' The woman addressing Silas would have been about Arthur's age, maybe a little younger, he figured. Only with some difficulty did he recognise in the lush bloated features that she had been a beauty in her day, the talk of the young men in all of the neighbourhood when he had been little more than a boy. If he remembered rightly, she had run away with a militiaman.

She continued. 'He was polite awright, our Arthur. Jus' his bad luck to run into them pressmen. Like as not he's sitting in some warm and foreign clime with lots o' servants an' no worries. Been missing him ever since.' The woman paused in thought, then from her toothless mouth burst the most jarring, heartless laughter. 'Been good for you though, him disappearing like that sudden like. An' him being sweet on your Margaret an' all …'

Silas Gregson's hands clenched to fists, but before he could express his anger he fell into another bout of coughing.

The landlord refilled his empty mug and said, 'You've got it bad today, Silas. You shouldn't be out with that cough o' yourn. You'll catch your death. An' there's a storm brewing.'

But the woman would not leave it alone: 'Must be an annivers'ry today, St Michaelmas Fair ...' she sneered and hiccupped. 'Wasn't that when young Arthur vanished? After the fair ...? Yeah, an annivers'ry today ...'

Young William Gregson had assisted his brother in manhandling their pigs into the market enclosures and helped him argue a good price until finally they had shaken hands on the deal and collected their money from the nail. Then he demanded his share of the money received and disappeared among the crowd of revellers at the adjoining fair. He was in luck. The pretty younger daughter of the local blacksmith seemed to be as pleased to see him as he was to see her. He spent his pennies, but whenever he tried to get a little personal she kept her distance and remained aloof. It was as if she was only biding her time. William could not believe that and the more she avoided him, the more urgent his advances became.

Until they chanced upon his brother. William wanted to pass by Arthur, who had gathered a small crowd as he wielded the weighty hammer and struck the plate that shot a bolt up to a bell. It rang out loud and clear among the tumult.

The blacksmith's daughter was delighted and wanted to stay and watch while William tried to pull her away. Arthur, recognising the young lady with his brother, immediately bowed deeply in the manner of a troubadour and with a slightly exaggerated gesture handed her the rosette he had just received as winning prize for his display of strength.

'To the prettiest girl at the fair,' he said. The girl blushed and William scowled and cursed under his breath.

'You better come quickly, young Arthur, your father … ' Arthur followed the swaying woman back to the inn, where his father had been taken ill with a coughing fit. They had called for the doctor, but he had only recommended rest with his usual medication. The old man was ordered home and to bed. For once Silas Gregson was too weak to argue and Arthur made him comfortable with fresh straw on the family cart. People promised to warn William of the turn of events.

The wind was stronger and Arthur hurried the horse back the long way to the farm and home. With the storm howling about them he had to concentrate, while on the cart his father babbled, mostly incoherent. Now he uttered feverish memories about the night his first-born came into the world. There had been a storm blowing that night too.

He remembered the candles guttering with the drafts that swirled about the old place and his wife, exhausted with the effort of bringing the lusty infant into the world, closing her eyes as she lay back against the pillow. 'Arthur …' She had breathed the word and startled him as he took the mewling child from old Mary Huggins who acted as midwife. 'Arthur … We will call him Arthur …'

'Arthur!' Silas shouted the word, frightening his son so that he whipped the horse on to greater haste. 'Nay, Silas. It will be Silas just as my father passed his name to me.' He shouted the remembered words in his agony. On the backboard his son did not understand.

Margaret had given him a look that broached no argument. Silas had looked down at the babe. For a moment he'd wondered if the child was something else he was going to have to hate his brother for … but the moment had passed. Watching a contented tiredness settle and relax his wife, he had concluded that women at times like these were not known to be rational. It was just a whim.

'Arthur it is then, my dear,' he had replied as he handed the boy back to old Mary and her swaddling blankets. 'Arthur … God rest him … it will be.'

Arriving home, young Arthur and his mother settled the heavily breathing and rambling man in his bed.

'It's early, still,' he suggested when all was done that could be done, '… think I'll ride back to the fair. I'll change the horse.'

'It's enough of a present to have the old man back, and you, safe and sound. Can't you stay now?' she pleaded.

'Mother, I promised a certain young maiden I'd take her to the dance,' was the answer. 'You'll want some help with all your chores sometime soon, won't you?' The mother wanted to ask questions as to what and who and … but her son was already out in the yard, chaining a fresh horse to the cart.

'Look after him, Mother,' he called back over his shoulder, 'he worries me.'

The hours went slowly, far too slowly for a mother fretting for the safety of her sons and with a sick husband to look after. When at last he fell into a fitful sleep, the waiting got worse. So did the wind, which now howled across the fields and treetops, and tore on the reeded roof as if it intended to raise it. The old wattle-and-daub house creaked and groaned under the onslaught and the strain on the well-pegged beams. The animals were restless in their stables and enclosures, their sties and coops. The animals always knew when something was not right.

'Lord,' she prayed, 'let us all get through this night in peace …'

She tried to keep busy, tried stopping herself from thinking, but to no avail. She let the fire be as the wind whistled down the chimney, blowing it out with its force. Just a storm lantern threw its sparse light about the simple room as at last she, too, fell asleep, overcome with worry and tiredness, her head in her arms, resting on the table. Her shadow darkened the walls behind her.

Tossing and turning in the marriage bed above her, her husband fought his own feverish battle with his memories and his conscience, 'Well, you had it all. And you had my woman. My Margaret. When she chose you over me that was the last straw. That's why I did it. You can see that, can't you, Arthur? It was the only way … So don't get Will to rout that tree …!' He came to a decision. He had to stop William doing his dead brother's bidding.

❖ ❖ ❖

'We're back, Mother, please go to bed now …' The urgent voice of Arthur close to her head woke the woman with a start. For a moment she was confused, then she smiled, 'You're back. Both of you. Why? What happened?'

'The storm, Mother. I'm surprised you could sleep through all the howling and blowing. Is Father alright?'

She nodded. 'He sleeps at last … but you, what happened?'

'Oh, the dance was called off with the storm. It's damaging houses and barns and people went home to look after their stock and their dwellings. We're lucky here. The woods protect us some.'

'If the woods are still here in the morning. We had to leave the cart. Made a detour – just managed to bring the horse around the fallen trees …' William sounded happy and helpful for once. 'We barely made it.'

'Go, tell her the news …' Arthur egged him on.

'It'll wait 'til the morning.'

Now the mother was anxious to hear what secret bound the boys together for once, though she, too, was tired and ready for bed.

Arthur was too excited, 'There may be two weddings soon. Go on, Will, you tell her.'

William grinned, 'The sly fox had kept it very quiet he was courtin' the blacksmith's daughter. Ursula, the elder one. So when I fell for the younger sister she seemed to be sweet on him too. Then I found out it was only because of her sister … I'm to be moving to the smithy quite soon.'

'My Ursula has been looking after her ailing mother. She wasn't even at the fair, but her sister can take over …' Arthur sounded like a very happy man.

The elation on the mother's face was almost tangible. There was to be no more enmity between her sons, 'Wait 'til I tell Father. No, I'll let him sleep. He'll be pleased in the morning.' At that moment a gust of wind shook the old house and made it sway with its force.

'The house will hold.' Arthur said confidently when he saw his mother's anxious look. 'It'll be here for many more generations, I hope.'

The fleeting shadow of worry left her face. 'We'll talk in the morning,' said the happy woman, as she climbed the stairs to her place beside her husband. 'Good night, both. Don't forget to douse the lamp.'

'Yes, Mother, we won't,' came two yawning answers.

A yell upstairs brought both the boys racing up the stairs. The sick bed was empty. 'He's not here. And nor are his clothes. He must have gone out when I slept. What's come over him?'

Where could he be?

The young men looked baffled. Then Margaret became rather serious, 'There is only one reason would make him get up and out on a night like this. He's out looking for you.'

William looked at Arthur, then at his mother, 'We must have missed him when we had to avoid the fallen trees. We'll clear them first thing tomorrow.'

'We better go looking. Get another lantern. With that chest of his it could be his ruin …' Arthur took charge as behoved the eldest son.

Margaret grabbed her shawl, 'I'm coming with you.'

'No, Mother,' said Arthur. 'Sorry, but you'll slow us down. We'll look after each other. You stay in case he returns before us. Have no worry on our part. We know these woods. We'll search the road to Burnt Wood. We'll take a horse each.'

It made sense. She would be a hindrance rather than a help on this stormy night. 'Now don't you worry. We'll find him.' There were no saddles, but the boys were used to riding bareback. Problem was to stay up when a gust of wind caught them unawares.

With the boys gone, Margaret shivered and pulled her shawl tighter about her shoulders. Her anxiety would not leave her. If only he had waited. Their sons were friends again. All was well. Then why did she feel so cold and so full of foreboding?

Silas Gregson laboured heavily with short breath and coughing fits, and a weakness in the limbs. He had not stopped to find a lantern for fear of waking his wife. She would not have let him go. He knew the way, even in the dark and the storm. In his feverish mind all the words said and all the looks and curses mixed and grew into a sense of dread. It must not happen! He must not let it happen! William must not cut down the tree! Not that tree! He would stop him. He had to stop him! His irrational action did not consider the hour of the night. There was only one thought: he must not fail. He struggled and picked himself up every time the wind threw him to the ground. His bones ached, his breathing rasped, his head hurt, he wheezed and stumbled until at last he stood in front of the tree of his nightmares.

Arthur and William had struggled all the way to the village, hanging on to their nags, practically laying on the manes, holding on, scrambling under and over fallen trees and fallen branches. Their father was not there. They retraced their search, cursing often when the elements combined against them.

They had exhausted every square foot, bend, dip and thicket along the road, when Arthur had an idea. 'What if,' he said, shouting over the wind, 'what if he's gone to the old grove? He seems to be obsessed by the place lately?'

It did not make sense, but then this was not a night like other nights and their father had acted strangely of late. Riding through the woods became increasingly hazardous. Whenever the scurrying clouds parted and the moon shone a pale light through the autumn trees, they realised the extent of the damage.

The brothers were leading the horses by the time they got to the sacred grove by the ancient earthen roundwall. It was a scene of carnage. Hardly any trees were left standing; some were splintered and broken, some simply torn from the forest floor. Almost everything bar the old stumps had been uprooted and flattened.

'He can't be here,' shouted William. 'Why should he be here?'

Arthur persisted, raising his lantern: 'He'd want to be with the Ancients ...' He did not know himself why he said it. Maybe it was the only thing that came to mind. He was trying to find the oak tree the old man had protected.

Suddenly he stopped.

Among the broken upheaval, the trees that had splintered and fallen under nature's onslaught, the light of his lantern fell on a gruesome sight. His father's eyes stared at him wide open from under a branch of the fallen tree. The branch had broken and pierced his chest. Blood gurgled from the open mouth that was trying to form words. Arthur bent low to listen to the babbling. The stark horror in those wide-open eyes drew him down and he had to look away as he lowered his ear. Words were coming like a spring from the earth, driven, awful words. Arthur wished he did not have to listen, but he could not pull away, either.

'I had to. Arthur, I had to. I loved her more than you …'

Silas was not looking at his son. He did not seem aware of his surroundings and his predicament. He was talking to someone who was not there. Or was he?

'I didn't want to kill you … I was no match … You gave me no choice … If I hadn't struck first … The acorn. I buried you like the Ancients … put an acorn under your tongue … I did the right thing, Arthur … Didn't I? I couldn't take you back and bury you at the church. It would have been wrong. There would have been questions …' The cruel words came faster and faster, turning into a torrent.

'Arthur, where are you, Arthur?'

Will's voice came closer, then seemed to be drowned out by the wind. Arthur could not find his voice. He wanted to yell, but his father's ramblings had terrified him. The meaning of the words began to sink into his numb and tired brain, when he heard another voice as from a great distance, 'There you are – what …?' William sank down beside his brother. He, too, was dumbstruck, at least for a moment. 'Father,' he yelled at last, 'why did you …?'

By the light of the storm lanterns the old man strained against the tree as if he wanted to shake it off. Arthur jumped up and tried to lift the splintered branch from his father's chest. His father rose with it, groaning and immediately Arthur stopped.

'You … got me now, Arthur … Your revenge … With Margaret … it was always you … but I … Curse you … I'm coming … to join you …' rasped the bloodied mouth.

'What? What's he mean?' yelled William, looking up at Arthur. But there was no need to shout. The storm had calmed. Blown itself out. Silas Gregson had fallen back to the forest floor and, but for the blood, he looked at ease.

Arthur knelt down beside him again. 'He wasn't talking to me,' he said with a faltering voice, 'he was talking to his brother. He is at peace now.' With that he reached down and closed the staring eyes gently with his shaking hand. 'He had to come here,' he said to William. 'It's where he buried Uncle Arthur. Fetch the horses … we need to get this tree off him. Our poor, poor mother …'

William rose silently from the heartrending scene, lifting his lantern to walk around the tree whose spreading roots had been torn up to a vertical position by the wind. Just then the clouds parted and a wan moon managed to eerily send its light down to the forest floor, where right under the centre of the raised mass of earth, among the tangled roots, a human skull glistened pale and peaceful.

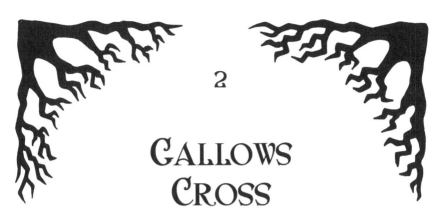

2

GALLOWS CROSS

U p on Gallows Hill, not far from where the windmill used to stand – the mill that killed its last miller – stood an old twisted cross. The wood had been cut and used green, hewn more than carved out of one odd-shaped trunk. Over time it had weathered until it resembled a forgotten road sign with one of the arms missing – or a gallows. Locally it was still called the Gallows Cross.

Why it was there nobody knew. It stood on an ancient roadway that had long been disused, the ancient thoroughfare little more than an overgrown footpath now. The story of whatever happened there or why it was erected had been forgotten over time, but not the feeling travellers experienced when perchance they had to pass near it. They always hurried away from it faster than they had approached, though nobody could account for why that should be.

There were rumours, tales that the older generation told down in the snug of the Miller's Arms over a game of Shove-Hap'ny or Nine Men's Morris, but nobody listened to them anymore. Certainly not the young people, the few that were left in the village, those that had not yet followed the exodus to towns and better employment.

Some locals said a witch had been burnt there back in the days when Bishop Bonner was keen on such activities. Others said

there had been a gruesome murder in that lonely spot when a desperate man had waylaid a merchant with money about him. Others insisted that it was the ghost of the last miller who was still haunting the area and that it had not been just a ghastly accident that had killed him; after the devastating flash fire there had not been enough of the miller to identify a cause of death ...

Whatever the reason, it was like an unwritten law that decreed avoidance of the old cross whenever possible. None of the locals would venture near it when the yellow broom swayed to the tune of the skylark, nor when the wind whistled in the heather and the crippled birches, nor when leaves were blown and swirled in mini tornados, certainly not on a night like this, when the mist rolled over the land and one could not see further than the dim lantern's immediate pool of light.

The mist pressed down on people caught outdoors as with an invisible weight, dampening sound and spirit and impressing a feeling of isolation, though at the same time one might encounter a fellow who was equally at a loss of directions. People would turn around frequently when the echo of their own footsteps tricked their self-assurance and it is perhaps not surprising that there were reports of ghostly sightings along the routes of the ancient highways on the heath.

Sometimes such wanderers would call in to the Miller's Arms for a pint or a tot of liquid courage before hastening on their way, so the landlord quite encouraged the stories.

That, at least, was the state of affairs when a one-armed stranger stopped in the village and looked up his sister on her small croft. Mavis Thornton, *née* Fuller, had been recently widowed and at first she was glad of the company. Even with only one arm a brother might be of help. He had left her alone to look after their ailing parents, and then the parents had died and Mavis had married a widower, old Fred Thornton. It seemed to be her lot in life to look after elderly and incapacitated relatives. Old Fred, too, had left this earth, but at least he had left her provided with a croft large enough to eke out a living.

Sam Fuller had volunteered for military service and had been in the thick of it, fighting the Turks at Gallipoli, but a bullet had shattered his arm and he had been retired and sent home. At the Miller's Arms he never shirked from telling his story.

Few in the small hamlet had ever travelled further than the fair at the next village, so the newcomer was looked up to by some for his worldly wise, much travelled past. Sam's damaged arm may have been a hindrance to work, but it did not intimidate his thirst, nor his flow of tales from his heroic exploits. That, and the dexterity he had acquired in his remaining arm that shamed many a two-armed man, had earned him a certain notoriety, a following almost, among the regulars of the Miller's Arms. He was entertainment and the more the ale flowed, the more he remembered

and the wilder his tales. Occasionally the landlord would even stand him a drink as a token of his appreciation to an old soldier, but there was something repetitive about the tales that somehow lacked on personal detail.

It was the eve of Halloween when the landlord of the Miller's Arms seemingly accidentally met Mavis Thornton outside the village shop on one of her rare expeditions from her smallholding. He'd had his suspicions for some time and he knew that Mavis was not one to mince her words, so here was his chance to prove his hunch. 'Morning, Mavis, you look in fine fettle. And how is the hero of the Dardanelles today?'

Mavis looked at him with a blank expression, as if he'd addressed her in a foreign tongue she did not understand.

'Your brother. He is one lucky soldier to make it back from Gallipoli, with all he's been through.'

Mavis sighed with understanding: 'Is that what he told you? Gallipoli? The Dardanelles? Him? Not very likely. He's been in jail locked up, not in no war. Is that what he told you? His arm was shot to bits during a botched robbery. Hero of Gallipoli indeed ...' Mavis Thornton was obviously unenthusiastic about her brother's return. He'd never before bothered with her or any of the family. Only when he had nowhere to turn had he remembered her and then he had proven to be of little help. On the contrary, work had never been her brother's strong point, not even when he had two arms.

The tale of Gallows Cross became the subject of conversation at the Miller's Arms again that evening. Here at least was something the locals could shine at and retell their tales and rumours and hints and suspicions. Few had personal experiences to impart, and those that had were prone to elaborate, nay, exaggerate. Blossom Flowerdew had been observed to walk miles out of her way to avoid the spot. Dogs would not retrieve any fowl shot on the heath that fell too close to the cross, and on one or two occasions the vicar had been called out to lay whatever spirit or spirits there were to rest.

As the ale flowed, so grew the stories.

The hero of the Dardanelles had been quietly listening to the conversations that were largely meant to impress him. But he was not impressed. Anyone who had faced the Turkish cannons and devastating shellfire of trench warfare and who had survived the sickness and inadequate medical service of that campaign would be made of sterner stuff. 'The dead on both sides lay so thick we had to negotiate a suspension of arms to clear them away – on both sides …' he had once insisted.

'Bet you never walked by the cross at night, though?' one of the revellers, Abe Martin, addressed Sam Fuller directly. 'I did once, when I had to go for the doctor at my wife's confinement.'

'You never,' contradicted Zach Williams, '… you borrowed our nag. An' her fetlocks were so dirty afterwards, you must 'ave ridden 'cross the fields rather than follow the hard path.'

'I did so! That way needs its ditches scoured, especially by yourn field. It's a mess when it rains …' Abe was prepared to back up his reputation with his fists and for a moment the situation looked like it might get out of hand.

'What do you mean by your insinuations?' Now Zach felt insulted.

'That is a bit needy, that …' Jack Salt piped up, but went quiet again when he caught a glance from the roused man.

'Gentlemen! Gentlemen!' The landlord tried to calm the situation. 'Do not insult a hero of our armed forces with such a trivial matter. The trenches of that faraway place did not intimidate him, I don't think so much as an old wayside cross would faze him.'

Sam Fuller raised his shoulders in agreement and downed the rest of his ale.

'Oh? Then let him prove it. If he's so darn heroic, let him go to the old cross.' Abe Martin had been riled and called a liar. He would not let it pass by as easy as that.

'Just 'cause you're afraid of the dark does not mean others are. Certainly not someone who has been out there and been shot at by Johnny Turk,' the landlord interceded.

'It's a silly argument, anyway,' Sam Fuller at last felt his chance to add to the conversation. 'Grown men afraid of their own shadow. Once you have spent your nights under the stars with dead and wounded all about you, you lose your fear of fairy tales.'

That did it. Abe wasn't having it. Being slighted and accused of being a coward, as he saw it, was one thing, but calling the reputation of the cross fairy tales, that was too much. 'Oh,' he said, '… the hour is soon approaching. Let any one of you go up to the cross and prove it.'

There was silence for a long moment while the landlord refilled their mugs. Nobody there would be so foolish as to put the old tales to the test. Slowly, one by one, they all turned and looked at Sam Fuller for a response.

The landlord made it for them, 'If it weren't such a silly idea, Sam here would probably be glad to show all of us how to handle a scary situation.'

'It's a silly idea all right. And I think it's about time I made my way back to my sister's. She'll be fretting …' With that, Jack fished and fumbled with his one hand in a pocket to find a coin to pay his slate. 'Think I'll have to owe you, landlord. No coin on me tonight.' Then he laughed a hollow laugh and added, 'Village gossip some people believe …'

'In that case you won't mind going that way home then?' said Abe.

'Yeah, no problem for you, passing that way, then?' added Zach.

Others just stared, waiting with some amusement.

'How would you know which way I go home in this fog tonight? Unless someone cares to come with me?' Sam opted for a counter challenge.

None of the late revellers were prepared to accompany him. It was the landlord's turn to make a suggestion, 'You could knock on it, then everyone here would know.'

'We wouldn't hear that here.' The smallish built Jack Salt piped up. As a carpenter's assistant he had the ideal solution. 'He could take some nails and a hammer and we'd hear him hammering them in.'

Meanwhile, Sam Fuller had been helped by the landlord with putting on his military greatcoat to keep out the cold on the way home.

'Hammer and nails? It's ridiculous. Where do you get a hammer and nails at this time of a night, so you can wake the dead and the whole village?' Scorn simmered in Sam's voice, as he was about to turn to the door.

Now the landlord interrupted: 'There's a job I meant to do. I've got hammer and nails right here, I think, just a minute …' He disappeared and returned with a hammer and a few good-sized nails.

'Bet he won't do it,' called one of the revellers.

Little Jack Salt almost stumbled over his own feet as he tried to get up to crow, 'Cock-a-doodle-doooo …'

Sam laughed, but not as confidently as he might have, 'How do you expect me to hold a nail and a hammer at the same time, even if I could see that silly road sign?' He had a point.

'Naaa … He's too scared to do it,' offered Abe.

'I know,' Jack had another idea, 'He could stick the nails in the cracks in the wood and then hammer them and if we don't hear it we can see them tomorrow …'

Sam Fuller accepted the nails and the hammer with poor grace. 'You better listen good … Night.' He turned to the landlord. 'An' you better set 'em up tomorrow. They'll all be losing their bets.'

With that, he stepped out of the door. His greatcoat flapped against his legs as it billowed out with his lengthening strides.

The company followed him outside, stumbling, but bringing their mugs, laughing sheepishly now. Jack attempted another cock-a-doodle, but it stuck in his throat now he stared into the swirling mist where the one-armed Sam had disappeared.

'Chicken, he?' Someone said, more as a statement than a question.

They were silent now as they listened for any noise that might penetrate the night. They almost fell over each other in surprise at the familiar sound of the church tower clock as it chimed out the twelve strokes of midnight.

'This is silly, think I'll wait inside, it's warmer,' said Jack, but he stayed all the same. The drink that had given them courage seemed to be losing its effect.

'Think I'll join you,' answered Abe. 'He'll never do it …'

At that moment they heard the distinctive sound of a nail being hammered in quick succession.

Then all was silent again.

'Never thought he'd do it,' said one of the revellers. They were sober now.

And they all left together, keeping each other company for as long as possible before each turned off to their beds.

Blossom Flowerdew came running in panic to the Miller's Arms, pulling up her skirts with one hand for extra speed. The spinster banged on the door as if pursued by all the imps of hell.

'The cross …' she shouted between taking great gasps of air, '… there's a body … I've seen it … with my own eyes … I've seen it … by the cross … there's been a murder.' She swooned and would have collapsed, had the landlord not caught her and pulled her inside, placing her on a chair by a table. 'You saw what? A body, you say?'

The woman looked up, quite obviously in shock: 'He's dead. Quite dead. Oh, it is awful …' She buried her head in her arms, as if trying to shut out what she had seen.

By that time a maid had joined them, staring open-mouthed at the woman at the table, 'What's awful? What happened?' she asked at last, when her employer put her in charge.

'Call my wife,' the landlord said. 'Give her a rum, not my wife, Blossom here, a stiff one, if necessary … and calm her down. She has seen something. Maybe it's nothing … I'm going to have a look.'

With that he left.

Farmer Zach Williams was already out in a field and Abe Martin was looking out of a window somewhat bleary-eyed when they saw the landlord of the Miller's Arms hastening in the direction of Gallows Cross. 'Come, have a look,' he shouted with foreboding, 'there may be something wrong.'

At the rare sight of the publican running, Zach left his horse standing in the field and went in pursuit and Abe was seen tucking in his shirt and lifting his braces over his shoulders as he rushed to follow them.

It was indeed a gruesome sight they found when at last they reached the Old Cross. Sam Fuller lay by the base of the cross, half in and half out of his greatcoat. Close-by lay the hammer.

His one hand clutched his heart, but it was his face that sent shivers down the spines of the witnesses. White as a sheet in death, his mouth open and contorted as in a silent scream, his wide-open eyes stared up at them, accusing. The way he lay was away from the cross, as if he had been trying to escape and was stopped.

'Look,' the landlord pointed to the cross. At about knee-height the greatcoat was attached to the gnarled wood by a nail that had been driven through the fabric. 'He must have …' The realisation silenced him.

'He must have thought he was grabbed by some devil or demon that pulled him back when he turned to get away …'

Abe finished his sentence for him. He shuddered. 'That would do for anyone.'

'His heart must have stopped in his fright.' Zach said to no one in particular, pointing to the arm that lay across the dead man's chest as if its fingers were trying to protect it.

'Can't have been easy, fumbling in the dark with one hand and a nail and a hammer …' admitted Abe.

The landlord shuddered, his conscience beginning to bother him, 'Close his eyes, someone, he seems to be staring at me.'

3

THE ANTIPODEAN GHOST

They were still dressed in their gaiters and jerkins, relaxed and leaning back in the stiff-buttoned armchairs, legs stretched out before them, their heads resting on the antimacassars, tumblers at hand and a bottle of brandy within easy reach. In the large if somewhat formal room, the dark oak panelling and the heavy carved furniture surrounding them added a sombre if masculine note, reflecting the stature and standing of the incumbent, the Reverend Archibald Jackson. A grand piano took up one corner and on one well-dressed desk a large, brass-mounted globe of tough brown papier-mâché underlined the world-wide interests of the learned owner, enhanced by a wealth of ancient books, manuscripts and rare illuminated tomes that inhabited the shelves, completely covering one of the walls.

The friends were silent for long moments – both musing on 'the-one-that-got-away', the biggest trout the stream had ever spawned to their knowledge – and the cleverest and most challenging. There wasn't much they did not know about fishing and the streams in this part of Essex. Certainly, the Reverend Jackson was well versed in local knowledge.

It had been a long time since their youthful friendship had been interrupted by life and led them to different parts of the country and to different callings, though at this moment that was far from their minds as recent events were proving to be the more compelling.

'I really thought I'd caught him this time,' mumbled the Reverend Jackson, more into his beard and his tumbler than to his companion, while swirling the precious liquid lovingly about the wide interior of the glass before moving it to his lips. 'To times past,' he nodded by way of a toast.

Dr Charles Carpenter removed the long curved pipe from between his teeth in order to reciprocate, just as the heavy brass knob of the door began to turn slowly but deftly. The door opened, creaking as it always did, then closed again, just as normally. Except, that is, no one had entered the room. Yet the footsteps that carried on and crossed over, past the two gentlemen and to the door on the opposite side of the study, belied that observation. There seemed to be a moment's hesitation as again the door handle was turned, the door opened and closed and the steps receded in the hall beyond.

The visitor had been about to lift his brandy glass with his free hand in reply to the offered toast with a well-remembered witticism from their college days, when his mouth remained open and the words remained unsaid. The barely held glass slipped from his fingers and bounced with a sharp, if melodious 'clink' on the floor. Though only the rim was broken, the precious liquid was spilled.

The host remained calm as a slight smile temporarily fluttered about his countenance. 'I wondered when you'd make the acquaintance of our resident ghost … Think nothing of it. He's quite benign, at least we think it's a 'he' – the weight of his footsteps leaves little doubt.'

'I … I …' The guest seemed to be taken aback, more so than others had been when suddenly confronted with the otherworldly occupant that shared the old rectory. He shivered, but regained his composure enough to reach down with some effort in an attempt at retrieving the broken glass. 'I am sorry. Not only do I spill your best brandy, I also break your glass – you should have warned me …'

'No matter, leave it for Mrs Heppleworth. She'll deal with it.' With that the reverend lifted and shook a small bell and a melodic tinkle rang out that could be heard on the other side of the Grange.

His guest still was ill at ease. 'It's suddenly got so cold. Is that a characteristic of your invisible lodger?'

Mrs Heppleworth entered presently, enquiring what might be required of her. 'I'm still basting the potatoes,' she breathed heavily, letting her employer know she had more to do than serving hand and foot on two relaxing gentlemen. Then she added with a less controversial tone, 'My, it's cold in here. I can't stop to lay a fire, not if you want to eat as well.'

The reverend apologised for interrupting her work, especially as he had worked up a healthy appetite with the afternoon's events. 'It's old you-know-who, Mrs Heppleworth, came passing through and upset our guest. I should have warned him. Just thought you'd like to know so the carpet gets the right treatment.'

The housekeeper wiped her hands on her apron and turned up her nose, indicating she was wise to their tipple. 'Brandy won't be seen on this colour.'

The guest, somewhat shyly and apologetic, handed the broken glass to the bustling woman and she accepted with poor grace. 'It's not usually this cold this time of an evening …' and she scuttled out of the door again.

'She is right, you know. Here, this'll put some colour back into your cheeks, Charles.' The reverend gentleman had replenished a fresh glass and handed it to his guest, adding, 'As house guests go, it's a rather benign presence. You'll soon get used to him. Mrs Heppleworth came with the living and she knew him long before I came on the scene. There's never been any bother.'

Almost at once the large papier-mâché globe slipped out of its fastening, rolled across the desk and bounced along the carpet, coming to rest near a window where it was lit by the last rays of the sun.

At this, even the confident Reverend Jackson was bereft of speech. With some effort, he managed to lift his tall frame out of the comfort of his chair and walk over to the brightly lit orb. 'That's just not possible,' he finally muttered under his breath, 'it couldn't jump out of its stand. That's solid brass …'

He tried to lift the large object, but it slipped from his grasp and rolled back into the light, the same continent illuminated just as before. Worry lines creased the reverend's forehead and his words came with some difficulty, as if he himself could not believe what he was saying, 'Australia. It's as if he wants me to look at Australia ...' With that he bent low and firmly gripped the object before returning it to the table and its brass stand, stoutly securing it with the fastening wingnuts, then turning it to inspect for any damage. Again it was Australia that faced him when finally the rotation stopped.

'Australia,' he said again, this time addressing his guest, 'Australia ...? Whenever I open an Atlas it opens at the page for the Antipodes. Whatever book I read, if it features Australia, that's where the pages open. What can it mean? I know little of Australia ... no connection? Do you?'

His guest pursed his lips and shook his head. 'No. No connection that I can think of ...' The friends sat silently for a while, both deep in their own thoughts, until Mrs Heppleworth announced that their table was laid.

As they rose from the comfort of the armchairs the reverend had arrived at a decision. 'There is an old man I met once near Chelmsford. I paid scant attention to him when he tried to tell me some tale he had heard about this very rectory. Perhaps I'll

look him up … if he is still alive. Aye, and I might look into another notion on my next visit to our great capital city … Have a rummage in old documents as I used to do in my younger days, when I was still going to astound the world with my knowledge and theories on history. I'd enjoy that. Yes, I think I will.'

In passing, he turned the globe back to bring his favourite country into view – England.

Doors opened quietly and candlelight flickered on the landing, throwing mysterious shadows over the darkly papered walls, dancing on the moulded plaster of the ceiling, moving as giant one-dimensional companions when all three of the house's occupants, rudely roused, collected at the top of the stairs in their bedtime attire. With the Reverend Jackson still wearing his night-cap and his friend still sporting the device intended to keep his moustache in good order, it was only Mrs Heppleworth who had stopped to protect her modesty and made sure she was wearing her dressing gown.

The unlikely trio just stared at one another in disbelief, then without another word, candles aloft, they descended the staircase, one hand each on the heavy banister, following the sound of a lilting piano tune that had roused them from their sleep. At the door to the study they stopped, preparing themselves to confront the intruder who had so ostentatiously interfered with the depth of their slumber. Still the musical interlude, played deftly by not quite the most accomplished hands, drifted loudly through the oaken door.

As lord of the manor, the Reverend Jackson led the charge, still carrying his candle if ever so slightly shaking. His free hand resolutely turned the brass handle of the familiar door, flinging it open as wide as his arm would allow. The candles flickered dangerously close to being extinguished, as three wide-awake rather pale faces stared with open mouths at the grand piano that stood silently and soundlessly where it always stood. All was quiet. No one sat at the well-carved swivelling stool, though the large triangular lid, which had been down to everyone's knowledge, was propped up as though playing was about to begin or had been in progress.

Even the Reverend Jackson reached up to close his nightshirt about his neck as the room's cold atmosphere gripped them through the thin fabrics of their nighttime attire. Sheepishly, they looked at each other. There was nothing to say. Had they dreamt it? There had not been time for anyone to leave the room between the sound stopping and the door opening ...

Once more, the enthusiastic sounds of the piano roused the sleepers that night, almost before their heads had been pressed back into their pillows. That time only the Reverend Jackson risked the descent to the study, making the sign of the cross before entering. As he'd expected, it was again silence that greeted him in the barely lit room. He said a short prayer, but as he was about to turn away again his eyes were drawn to the orb of the globe. As he walked over to it, he remembered exactly how things had been before he and his guest retired. It had been England that he had left uppermost in his line of vision, not Australia ...

Several months had passed before the Reverend Jackson asked his friend of old, Dr Charles Carpenter, back for a visit, stating some mysterious developments in his letter and hinting at some very telling discoveries.

It was a somewhat distraught and dishevelled Charles who arrived at the rectory on the hill by coach, the horses flecked with foam from their exertions, their legs coated in mud almost up to their bellies.

'Heaven save us, Archibald,' the welcome guest continued once he had greeted his old friend. 'You'll have to do something about those roads hereabouts. They're almost impassable in this weather. At one time the mire came up to our axels. The horses barely managed. But enough of my travails, what of these mysterious secrets I am to be party to?'

'Oh, that can wait, old friend. You want to see our roads in winter … I'll have to remind Farmer Golding that it's his turn to harrow the roads. But, you must be famished after your journey. Mrs Heppleworth has laid the table and we daren't disappoint her. We'll take the rods down to the river after lunch. We'll talk then …'

Some time later, the Reverend Jackson led his companion via the churchyard, where, he assured his guest, the first of the clues was to be found. It all revolved around previous incumbents at the rectory, husband and wife and their only daughter, Rachel. The rector's opulent grave lay in the shadow of a sturdy buttress close to the church, together with his wife's, but there was no grave or marking for a daughter. This had puzzled the current incumbent for some considerable time and had been spoken of by some of the older folk in his parish, even before his recent search for the facts.

Rachel had been a quiet girl with simple tastes in spite of her pampered, if solitary, upbringing. Loving music and quiet rides in the countryside, she never seemed to mix with the youth of her age and her parents' circle of friends. Instead, she had developed a deep and abiding passion for the boy who dared not look on her as her equal. An ostler … he was just an ostler, there to look after the horses, the stables and the gardens of the rectory. A labourer, unable to read or write, as compared to the private schooling of the rector's daughter. It was he who would saddle up her horse for a canter in the deep lanes and across the parish fields. Occasionally he had been able to advise her, or suggest likely rambles with his knowledge of the neighbourhood.

Quite regularly, she would play the grand piano and her tunes might carry across to where the boy was working. Every note, every sweet melody would be ingrained in his receptive brain. He would hum the tunes, but only out of earshot of her father.

Her mother was a quiet lady, not a match for her father's stance: 'I am not wasting all that education on my daughter so she can sweep up some worker's hovel. And to produce more of their uncivil brats …'

Of course, he would not say this within earshot of any one of his flock, only to his meek wife. Though some of his parishioners were aware of his unchristian, arrogant ways, he was the rector and no one would have the will or the nerve to challenge him on his private views.

When, in her father's view, it became obvious that his daughter would not settle for any of the eligible bachelors in the diocese worthy of her hand, it was the young ostler who was sent away to work for an old acquaintance of the rector. This acquaintance was a man who could be counted upon to work the boy all the

hours of the day and night, to drive out any such notions he might have about the girl and keep him firmly in his place. Outwardly, the rector went to some length to indicate to all and sundry that it was in the boy's best interest to be apprenticed and to learn a trade that would improve his station in life. Some sceptical eyebrows were raised as to the suitability of the slight boy for the life of a thatcher, though it was none of their business.

The girl pined away, withdrawn and listless, shunning company and, it appeared, preparing herself for the life of a nun. Even her music fell silent, as she contained herself with the scales she was ordered to practise. Then, one day in the midst of spring, when lambs gambolled in the meadows and birds sang their little hearts out announcing the coming of a new generation of wide-beaked chicks, her attitude changed. Her pallor improved, colour came back to her cheeks, the sparkle returned to her eyes and she was observed skipping as she walked along.

Her mother, who had suffered with her in sympathy, wishing a life of love for her daughter instead of the loveless marriage she herself had to endure, realised it first. Eventually her father, too, noticed the change. His enquiries very soon resulted in an answer. The ostler boy had escaped his enforced indenture and absconded from the thatcher's rule. He'd found gainful employment at a kindly farmer's home in a neighbouring parish. The rector did not confront his daughter with the story, instead he lay in wait for her as she silently unlatched her window in the still of night and escaped, directly into the arms of her waiting lover.

Enraged, the rector attacked the smitten boy, commanding his daughter back to the house and marching her love off to the constable's house to spend the rest of the night in the stocks. Bundled back indoors, the girl was at first given into the care of her mother, but when she took the girl's side and threatened suicide unless her husband relented, the rector took personal charge and accompanied the silent girl by stagecoach to his sister's home in Hampstead, London, the very next morning. There, it was made known, she was to learn social graces and enjoy better schooling as befitted a young woman of her qualities.

The boy was accused of theft when an ancient twisted copper torc was found on him, an armband the rector recognised as belonging to his daughter. At first the constable was sceptical, but the rector insisted the villain had been found outside the rectory that night with theft in mind – the proof was there, in his pocket. Had he not absconded from his indentured place of employment for just that reason? The boy's pleas of innocence and his story of the torc being a love token freely given to him by the girl was simply not believed, nor was his statement that he had never entered the rectory except in the course of his duties while he was employed there. When he insisted the girl had joined him of her own free will, he was taken from the court and bundled straight into the court's jail for such blasphemous words. Such was the rector's influence; the boy's sentence was transportation to the other side of the known world, to be carried out with immediate effect.

It had been a miscarriage of justice, everyone in the ostler's family had agreed, but there was nothing to be done – the law took its course. For several years the family heard nothing from the boy, but when they did it was by letter, astonishingly in the deportee's own hand.

'So he had learnt to write either on the journey or in the confines of an Australian prison? That's hard to believe! He must have been of special intellect?' Dr Carpenter interrupted the rector's flow of words.

'Oh, yes, that would seem to be the case. He certainly wasn't the villain he had been painted in court.'

Leaving the churchyard, the friends continued in deep conversation along the winding path to the river, their walk only punctuated by stops to share the contents of the reverend's hip flask.

They had waded into the slow-flowing stream, each concentrating on their task in hand, once again the rivals they had been in younger years, when Charles Carpenter took his mind off his fishing rod for a moment. Turning to his friend, he asked, 'And how have you learnt all this since our last meeting?' just as his line stretched taut and his rod almost slipped from his hand. There followed one mighty tussle between man and trout, which caught the good doctor off balance, resulting in a headlong dive into the surprisingly sobering waters.

Floundering, he nonetheless held on to his rod with grim determination. Grabbing the net, the Reverend Jackson was by his side as quickly as the swirling water would allow and between them they reeled in the largest, stoutest fighting fish they had seen – it just had to be 'old faithful' … at last.

The Reverend Jackson almost felt cheated out of his prize, so often had he attempted to reel in the patriarch of the river. Fishing in future would be an anti-climax. To be beaten to it by an old friend was small consolation. It was difficult to concentrate on the story he had mulled over in his mind these past months. While they admired the catch of the season, the friends rested against a spreading willow on the riverbank.

'We had better give Mrs Heppleworth a chance to prepare your prize catch. And you need to get out of those dripping wet clothes, my friend, or you might have to call on yourself for a cure.' They headed back to the rectory. 'You asked how I came by the story, Charles.'

'And I am wondering just why it should be of interest to me? But no doubt I shall find out in good time.' The doctor chuckled, as he handed back the shared flask.

'Well, much of it comes from past conversations, but once my curiosity was roused, I began to ask questions and I had a stroke of luck when I found Harry Burchill, the son of the deported ostler's brother, who farms a large spread near Chelmsford. His father, Harry Senior, has alas departed from this world. Young Harry Burchill is a diligent and likeable fellow, as behoves someone of that family. He was pleased to impart all he knew of his uncle's misfortunes. William Burchill had returned a bitter man, who hardly ever spoke of his experiences in the Antipodes.'

'Ah, so he did return?'

'Oh, yes, but not until the full fourteen years of his sentence had been served. He had been of independent means, though, as his education had allowed, but he never married. By the time of his return, the girl's aunt in London had been widowed and joined her brother, to look after him here at the rectory. When Will Burchill returned to his former workplace he was told the girl had died while at school in London. The girl's mother had, it was said, died of a broken heart at losing her daughter, though some hinted that in reality she had taken her own life.'

The Reverend Jackson had to stop for breath temporarily, but that did not stop his flow of words for long.

'The young fellow had gained an education out in the colony of Sidney Harbour's Cockatoo Island, when he was given the freedom of the colony for good behaviour, as I found out later. But back to the former convict's return: he had secured a position of some trust with a college in Oxford, but that had not suited him, as he was far too restless and forever searching London for his lost love. Eventually he returned to his earlier training with horses and became a long-distance coachman for the mail service. That would have given him more chances to scour London and all over the eastern counties. It was his misfortune to be killed when he stood up to a highwayman close by Epping Forest. His body has never been found.'

Dr Carpenter was beginning to feel the discomfort of walking in damp clothing.

All the same, there were more revelations from the reverend sleuth's searches in the London archives. A William Burchill was listed among the passengers of a schooner that arrived from

Sydney, Australia. According to the ship's log, he accompanied the governor's two boys on their journey to England as a kind of chaperone, as the boys were to attend university at Oxford. So it would have been an arrangement of trust. It even had the actual signature of William Burchill.

'Perhaps he taught himself, but there is a note among the papers stating that the children's guardian was to be afforded every assistance in his and their studies and comfort while on board.'

Then the rector had had another stroke of luck. Among the brittle documents was found an earlier letter from the governor of the colony addressed to lawyers in London, which contained a specific request for a pardon and assistance for one convict who had been instrumental in the rescue of the governor's sons when they had become involved in a deadly incident in the harbour. The reason for the incident was not explained and the good rector suspected a prank, but the letter did not stint in its praise of the outstanding good nature of the convict, one Will Burchill, who had rescued the children almost at the cost of his own life, while other convicts had jeered at the difficulties the boys had found themselves in. The letter also stated that the said Will Burchill steadfastly declared his innocence.

Mrs Heppleworth was totally unimpressed by the large catch she was expected to prepare for supper that evening. Instead, she insisted on serving the meal she had prepared, though as the next day was a Friday, she would serve the gentlemen's prize as the main meal.

During supper the Reverend Jackson complained bitterly about his persistent problem with the accursed gout and the good doctor prescribed both syrup and wine of colchicum as the latest remedy in the treatment of the problem.

It was some time later that evening when again the two friends were ensconced in their respective well-upholstered armchairs in the rector's study, that the subject of Will Burchill was raised once again.

The story was now advanced by an unlikely source and the proud sleuth was telling it with some relish. Whilst in London he had also been lucky enough to trace the daughter of a wet nurse, a lively, out-going woman whose mother had formerly been in service to the old rector's sister. With money received, which, so the reverend sleuth surmised, had been generous in order to buy her silence, the former servant had set up her seamstress business in Covent Garden, a task that her daughter now happily continued to pursue. Luckily, the daughter had not felt bound by her mother's promise of silence, for it continued the story of the hapless Rachel in London.

In Hampstead the girl had sickened and had taken abed with a fever, though as the weeks and months went by it had become obvious there was more to her 'sickness' than had at first been recognised.

When the baby was born it was small and sickly, but it clung tenaciously to life against all expectations. The young mother was not so determined and all the best doctors her aunt might consult could not replace with medicines the suffering of her broken heart. She died, having held her baby just fleetingly. Interred in London, her body had not even been returned to the home she had once loved, while a wet nurse had to be found to take her place in the nursery. It was the daughter of that wet nurse who had recounted her mother's memories.

The baby boy, the reverend recounted, had been adopted into a family of some substance, though without the revelation of any of the child's history. The former wet nurse had kept a distant and tactful eye on the youngster, who had grown up in a loving family and eventually studied the mysteries of medicine.

'Oh, no …' Dr Carpenter was beginning to realise where his friend's words were leading. He had been told little of his origins, except that his real mother had died in childbirth. Nothing more was known of her. Strangely the small copper object he had always worn on a strip of leather about his neck seemed to grow warm against his chest. Instinctively he put his hand to where it lay beneath his shirt.

'The only connection was an ancient torc, which the mother had placed by the child's cot before she died,' the rector went on to explain. 'That token had been saved by the midwife attending his birth and passed on to his adopting family and had later become his constant companion.'

The guest had been silent, deep furrows lining his forehead as he realised what his friend was about to say.

'Do you still carry that torc about your neck, that used to give us such hilarity when we insensitive lads teased you so mercilessly at the old school dormitories, Charles?'

Dr Carpenter sat pale and stoney-faced in his chair, the cut-glass brandy goblet not passing to his lips. Instead, frozen in mid-air, the pressure that the white knuckles and iron grip exerted suddenly shattered the glass in his hand, waking him as from a deep trance, the hand dripping glass and brandy and blood.

Once they had attended to the cut hand under the doctor's own instructions, Mrs Heppleworth saw to the glass and the carpet, while footsteps were heard all over the house and doors were opened and closed and banged indiscriminately.

'Do us a favour, old friend,' said the Reverend Jackson wistfully, just before they retired for the night. 'Leave that torc on your bedside table tonight, just to be sure.'

That night the tunes emanating from the study were of a jolly sailor type, sea shanties and songs of work on the sea, joyous and unconstrained, but nobody left their beds to investigate.

By the time Dr Carpenter was ready to return home the weather had changed quite unexpectedly. From his high bench the coachman whipped and hurried the horses as best he could, trying to reach better roads before the storm broke. It was not to be. Lightning lit the darkened sky and thunderclaps broke directly above them with a sound that was almost physical. Out in the open they were exposed to the full gust of the wind that threatened to overturn them, were it not for the misery of the cloying Essex clay that sucked at wheels and hooves, as if wanting to hold on to them. The deep ruts into which the wheels sunk did not augur well for axels and spokes and

the rain driving almost horizontally now added its misery to the quagmire. The lone passenger being buffeted and thrown about in the coach was torn between commanding the coachman to spare the horses and the desire to hasten the journey.

Presently lightning blinded man and beast, striking its fiery force into one of the towering elm trees that lined the route just ahead of them, the very air bristling with electricity. The coachman pulled on the reins, yelling at the horses, just as the cataclysm of the sound added its ear-shattering momentum. The frightened horses instead burst forward, entangling the chains that held them to the whippletree and stopping again as if fighting an invisible foe, neighed wide-eyed, reared and punched at the air with their front hooves. The wheels had slipped into one of the deepest ruts on the highway, threatening to pull the carriage apart.

At the same moment a fiery arrowbolt from the dark sky above them split a tree asunder, which threatened to crush the now stationary travellers.

It was at that desperate point that a calm suddenly descended on the shivering animals, that the chains were sorted almost calmly as they stepped back and turned about as if guided by invisible hands. Smaller branches whipped the rear of the turning coach as the large elm – bursting, crackling and burning – smashed into the road immediately behind them, missing them by seconds.

Next they were hurrying back towards the bend in the road, where a sharp turn in the opposite direction led them back to the village on the hill and towards the stables of the rectory, where a grateful Dr Carpenter apologised to the surprised reverend for imposing on his hospitality just a little longer.

'It's ... it's as a miracle,' wheezed the relieved coachman, still out of breath from his own exertions. His hands were raw from pulling on the reins. 'I couldn't hold them darned hosses. Nor move 'em. It's as if someone was handling them by the bridles with invisible hands. Someone with great skills an' darin'. I thought we were all going to die for sure.' He shook his head, trying to fathom what had happened. 'A miracle. Definitely a miracle.' He kept repeating those words.

'It was someone with great skill with horses who saved you,' observed the Reverend Archibald Jackson with a laconic smile while the horses were being stabled and the coach secured until the weather passed and his guest could depart in safety, 'An ostler, someone who knew horses for a living.'

Then he looked directly at Dr Carpenter and added thoughtfully: 'Someone who had to save his son.'

4

MURDER ON THE MARSH

You can't murder a dead man, can you ...?

How long had he been floating out there, in the convoluting runnels that fill and empty with the tide, bony fingers trailing in the water, arms outstretched like the crucified Lord, but face down, so that at first it looked as if his head was missing? His skin, where it was visible, was the colour of veined, almost transparent, blue-white parchment. His chest was held up

by a long fowling gun, the business end of which pointed aimlessly across the punt's bow to the pale horizon.

How long had his slim and shallow craft bobbed on the tides, swirled around and nudged against the tassocks in the half-land where he was – where he had been – quite at home? His jerkin had been disturbed, his braces were taut and by the droppings it was apparent that a seagull or two had been perching on the hilt of the solid, well-made knife that stuck out from his back, close to his heart. There was little blood.

Sam Felgate pushed up the rim of his black hat and scratched his head. What was he to do? His immediate instinct told him to pass blindly by. Getting involved could only lead to trouble. The man was obviously dead. There was no more to be done for him now. Except by a priest? The authorities might as soon as not pin the foul deed on him. Even without turning him over and seeing his face, he recognised the deceased. Everybody knew everybody out here on the marshes.

'That's Eph Woods.' He thought aloud. 'I'd know those braces anywhere.' Many a pint of small beer had he drunk with Eph Woods, who was never happier as when he could be out here alone on the marshes at all hours, but best afore sunrise, when the moon was just a sickle and the horizon barely visible in anticipation. But he had not been there entirely to listen to the dawn chorus, Sam mused. Eph Woods had been the most skilled and the most successful punt-gunner in the marsh. Why, he held the record for the most geese downed with one barrel of shot in all of the Hundred of Barstable.

The familiar sound of a pair of geese squawking as they passed overhead barely registered into his deliberations.

'Hullow, Samuel, are you saying a prayer or have you found the gate to the underworld?' The voice, so close to him, made Sam jump almost out of his boots. So deep in thought had he been, he had not heard the approaching footsteps. As his body swung around, he recognised the dark and familiar person of the parson.

Now it was too late.

The parson had approached close enough to witness the cause of Sam's conundrum. 'Oh, my God, *ad misericordiam*,' was all

the usually vocal servant of the cloth could utter as his right hand instinctively rose and hastily made the sign of the cross.

Looking extremely sheepish, Sam offered his knowledge: 'It's Eph Woods, Reverend, from Haddon. He must 'a been out here some time an' the tide brought him to the wall …'

'Good heavens, man, get him out of there and bring him up here. It's the least we can do as Good Samaritans.' He spoke in the plural, but made no attempt to go down and help personally.

Sam stalled. He wasn't too keen on the idea of slithering down from the sea wall into the briny. He'd detected a not too unfamiliar odour coming from that direction when the wind turned. 'What about the law, Sir, shouldn't we wait and not tamper with the evidence?'

'*Sic transit gloria mundi.* For pity's sake, man, it's a fellow human being. Or was …' He, too, had now detected the proof of the frailty of humankind passing on the air, though he did not show it, except for bringing a kerchief unobtrusively up to his nose. 'Perhaps you better hurry and alert the constable, forthwith.'

Then he suddenly bent forward and, shakily, pointed at the knife. 'I know that knife … Oh my God … That's …'

Sam stood there, open-mouthed, waiting for the words to follow. His curiosity was roused, but nothing further came from the parson's lips than a groan. Then, as Sam still lingered in anticipation, the man of the cloth turned on him, exasperated. 'The constable. The sheriff. Anybody! For God's sake, hurry, man.'

That was enough. He obviously was not going to discover to whom the knife belonged – not yet, anyway. As he turned reluctantly to get back to the village on his unforeseen errand, another shout from the parson immensely accelerated his strides, 'Hurry, Sam Felgate, unless you want to be blamed for the death …'

There was nobody about at the old wharf, nobody that could be seen, anyway. The familiar barge of the Howard family looked deserted. That was unusual to Sam, who had started to shout from some distance, at least as loud as his strained lungs would allow. He shouted again at the boarding plank, as he leant against a post, trying to regain his breath and loath to cross over on to what was, after all, private property.

But there was no reply.

Annoyed, he shouted louder in case everyone was asleep, though that was unlikely in daytime. Bert Howard's son, young Bert, could have hurried for the constable and saved him the walk. Not a sound, except the creaking boards and the eerie sighs of the timbers as the waves gently pushed against the hull and in turn released it in its muddy berth. The constant rhythm of the moving barge played on his nerves.

Dogs had started barking at the nearby farm, alerted by his shouts. Still there was no reaction. Apart from animals, the farm also seemed deserted. There was no alternative but to hurry on.

Sam Felgate staggered up the slope, hastened along the slippery track straight into The Barge Inn and collapsed. 'On the seawall … the parson … dead in a punt … hurry … get the blacksmith … cunstable …' His voice failed him and ended in a strangled sound, as he gripped his throat and collapsed on to an offered stool.

'Here,' said the innkeeper, 'wash your throat and start again. That's better. So the parson is dead in a punt on the seawall?'

Sam handed back the empty mug of ale with trembling hands, then wiped a shaky fist across his mouth, still fighting for breath, but now a little less agitated. 'No, not the parson. Eph Woods. Must have been out there for days. Uuugh.' He shook his shoulders. 'Recognised him by his braces. Dead as a doornail.'

The publican pressed another steadying mug into his shaking hands. 'If he's dead, where's the hurry?'

Sam croaked, 'The cunstable … must get the cunstable…'

The landlord was still confused. 'Who did you recognise, the parson or Eph Woods?'

Sam realised he was not getting anywhere. He'd have to go himself. 'The parson knows who did it. The knife …' With that he stumbled to his feet and made for the door.

'That will be two farthings,' said the landlord calmly but deftly, 'for my best ale,' and he barred the way.

'But, I thought … You're interfering with the wheels of justice. Got to hurry. The parson …'

'The parson can wait.'

Sam Felgate scrabbled around in his pockets: 'No coin on me. Will have to owe you.' With that he pushed past the rotund man and hurried towards the smithy.

It was the blacksmith's lot to have been elected constable by the Vestry meeting on account of his size and his helpful nature. By the time he arrived at the scene the Vesper bell was ringing.

'Sorry, Reverend, Sir, had to borrow a horse from old Tom afore coming out here,' he shouted from some distance when he noticed the parson coming rushing towards him.

'Good God, man, what kept you? I'll be late for service. Couldn't leave the dead unguarded, could I?' With that the red-faced man rudely and hastily brushed past the constable and the horse and hurried towards the sound of the bell.

'Sam Felgate said …' The constable stopped himself as he realised he would get no answer. Then, grumbling to himself, he continued, 'Why is it always me who gets to do these jobs? Because no one else is dumb enough.' He answered his own question, then mumbled, 'Be calm. It's what cunstables do.' He kept on mumbling profanities under his breath, sentiments quite dark and unexpected from the usually gentle blacksmith. Sam Felgate, too, had been in a hurry to catch up with some unspecified urgent job.

A small crowd had gathered at The Barge Inn by the time the constable returned, dragging the flimsy boat complete with its tragic contents behind the horse. 'For evidence,' he said, almost officially. 'Too late for a doctor. Best take him straight to the carpenter.'

'Who is it?' enquired Mary Sloane, who always lagged a little behind everybody. Pushing through the crowd and pointing her clay pipe, she called out, 'Looks like Eph Woods by his trousers. What's he doing with a knife in his back?'

All the same, the carpenter had called the doctor when he'd found a strange mark on the body of the deceased.

'Well,' said Dr Winthrop with some gravity, '… a tattoo. Curious. The deceased seems to have been a mariner at some time. I shall have to look it up in my notes. Maybe some secret society, or the like I've never heard of. In my time as a naval doctor I've seen some strange things, but I've never before seen this one. Curious. And there is something else that's strange. That knife. There is no blood about the knife … The deceased did not die of the knife wound. That was added later. Maybe to divert attention? Or by someone else?'

With his thumb pressing his nose and his hand covering his mouth, his words sounded strangely forced.

'But,' mumbled the carpenter, '… about that knife. You can't murder a dead man? Can you?'

'Well, abrasions around the neck show he was strangled. Hmmm,' Dr Winthrop rubbed his chin and added another observation, 'Strangled by a very large pair of hands it would seem. Or two?'

And thus the learned man departed in deep contemplation.

There was an additional complication, or was it a clue? Eph Woods had not been found in his own punt, but in that belonging to the Fothergill brothers.

All manner of theories began circulating about the village and its neighbourhood. 'A large pair of hands …' the doctor had said. Or perhaps two smaller pairs? Or more? A tattoo? Nobody had known about that. A secret affiliation? Speculation was rife, yet the case remained unresolved. The funeral was arranged two days later, with the cheapest coffin, but the largest crowd the village churchyard had accommodated for a very long time.

Slowly the villagers settled down to business as usual, but the event was not forgotten. Far from it. At The Barge, at the grocers' shop, wherever people met, suspicions were aired with winks and hints added. Some remembered a long-standing whispered suspicion of a possible dalliance by Eph Woods with a spinster in the village. Had the lifelong bachelor led on the single woman with promises of respectability? She had been acting very secretive for a long time, but then she suddenly had not had a good word to say about him. Salome Sterk had remained a spinster and she had been among the women tidying up after a hog roast evening that night. She could have taken the knife …

But the knife had not killed the wildfowling bachelor, the doctor had said. Then again, Salome Sterk lived in the direction of the spot where the dead man had been found.

Village tongues, once roused, can make mountains out of molehills.

It was a long walk to the well for most of the women from the widely dispersed dwellings with their buckets and pitchers, but the well had become the hub of village gossip. What The Barge was to the menfolk in the way of discussing local and world events, or what passed for the events in their world, the well was to the women, or at least to those who still dared to go outdoors for fear that they, too, might encounter the murderer of Eph Woods.

There was no talk of strangers having been seen, so one of them must be a murderer. But who?

Mary Sloane had thought about it for some time while quaffing away on her clay pipe. Then her eyes lit up and she remembered something else. 'Sal,' she said, 'Sal had the knife. She was takin' it back to the parsonage with her, little goody-goody … Oh, no! Then she must have …? But she used to be sweet on 'im she was.'

'Who? Her? Salome Sterk? The parson's daughter? But butter wouldn't melt in her scrawny little mouth. Her sweet on Eph Woods?'

'Yes, so she was, but she couldn't have killed and carried 'im. Not 'im as a dead weight. More likely two big lads. Much more likely the Fothergill twins …'

The widow Fothergill had approached quietly and unnoticed with her water pitcher.

'Oh, dear,' one of the assembled women put her hand to her mouth as if to stop herself from saying something unspeakable, while her eyes rolled in her head towards the just arrived widow.

All eyes turned to Mother Fothergill, who had heard enough to understand the drift of the conversation, 'Eph Woods? But I seen him with the cunst'ble after the celebrations, that night after the queen's party. They was arguin' fit to bust. But they wus nowhere near Hall Marsh. Went towards Dutch Marsh.'

The widow Fothergill was a light sleeper; most everyone knew that. Sometimes at night she was seen in the lane leading to the inn. Ghostlike she would glide into the shadows whenever anyone approached. Her sons frequented the house of iniquity far too often for her liking and she could not or would not sleep until they had laid their heads down on their sparse cots in her small cottage. Then she would lock up, blow out the candles and head for her own truckle bed. Her sons, in their efforts to avoid being the catalysts of village jokes, took it upon themselves to drag out the homeward journey most evenings, in their minds to prove their independence and manhood. Whenever anyone hinted at the subject, they would get into fights.

Now the whispers of their involvement would not cease. How could they explain that Eph Woods' body had been found in their punt in their favourite fowling area?

'Ah, yes, that's what people say, too, but then how could he be found in your punt at Hall Marsh?' Mary Sloane stuck out her chin and stared directly at the widow Fothergill. She'd always fancied herself as a bit of a sleuth.

The women could not think of a solution, so it came back to the brothers.

Obviously the widow was only protecting her sons, even if her sons had not been seen with Eph Woods. Neither did they have any business with him nor reason for strife. But people have long memories. Liza Howard remembered them out on the marsh with their guns. Out on Hall Marsh.

The widow was getting desperate: 'Eph Woods liked to go to Dutch Marsh an' that's where the Joneses from over Northwick like to shoot.'

Perhaps they had eliminated another wildfowler? Or got into an argument? Perhaps one of them had strangled Eph and the other had then added the knife? Eventually the Joneses of Northwick were mixed up with the Fothergill brothers.

Yet always the argument came back to her sons. 'My boys wouldn't do that,' insisted the widow. 'And they were home early that night.'

'But we don't know when Eph Woods was killed, they could have gone out on another night. How else would he get into your punt?'

'Well, I'm not leaving the house in the evening until we know ...'

The conversation was going round in circles and in her anxiety to steer suspicions away from her sons, as she saw it, she made a desperate statement: 'No. No. You don't understand. I did it. I. Me.' The way she insisted it seemed she was proud of her action. Except that it was not possible.

'But you were nowhere near there, nor on any other night. Unless you can fly? On your broomstick? You were seen hiding in the shadows up by Old Sam's barn, waiting for your boys as usual. Where's your broomstick? Hey?' Mary Sloan would not let her take the blame. The widow was too well known in the village for waiting for her sons at night. Too many people had seen her.

This was a distinctly unhealthy turn of events for the old woman, to be accused of witchcraft. Even in Queen Anne's days this was still a punishable offence and not to be invited. But she wanted to protect her boys. They were all she had left from a large family. Her husband had never been any good when he was alive. He'd always preferred the inn, even when there was work to be had. The girls had married away and had their own families to look after. The boys were all she had left. If an accusation of witchcraft was to be raised against her, so be it.

When she'd filled her bucket at the well, she had to make a great effort to transport it. Even so, much of it was spilled.

'You strangled a grown man with your little hands and put him in your boys' punt when you can't lift a small bucket?' queried Liza Howard to general laughter.

'Oh,' sighed the widow, 'I'm strong when I really try.'

The idea was so unlikely, one of the women tried to change the subject, 'You're no stronger than the parson's daughter an' she had a knife and she was sweet on the wildfowler.'

'Salome? The parson's daughter? Don't know about that, but the blacksmith was hankering after her. Quite the wrong sort of wife for a blacksmith with her airs and graces, but there is no accounting for taste. Not when it comes to besotted men. He really pined for her like a puppy, the big fellow.'

'Well, the blacksmith has large hands.'

'No, he never, he's such a big softy. Remember how he cried when his dog died? That Irish wolfhound that allus followed him around everywhere?'

'Ah, but he has taken to drinking since the murder. He's hardly left The Barge, I've heard.'

'Wouldn't you after what he had to collect in that punt?'

The women were certain they knew their village. It always came back to the Fothergill brothers. Couldn't two pairs of hands look like one large pair?

The snug at The Barge was the favourite watering place for the village elders, with some future elders added in. Visibility was hampered by thick smoke from the several clay pipes rising to the low-beamed, dark-stained ceiling, swirling about the beams whenever anyone moved. Beyond the crackling fire lay the Pump Room, which shared the fire's heat, but was frequented mostly by younger or less eminent members of the community. Or by strangers. The open fire both divided and joined the separate spaces, which had their individual entrance doors from the outside.

'If I remember rightly,' the churchwarden carpenter said by way of attempting to solve the mystery, 'he came here maybe more than twenty years ago, someone's relative, I think. The old vicar's maybe? The old vicar had some curious friends back from his mission. Took him a long time to settle in, took Eph Woods, but never really was one of us. I mean, not really. Kept hisself to hisself, at least in the beginning. Now later … lately he took to drink a lot. Then he could be quite cantankerous. It's odd, though, him being found at Hall Marsh. Wasn't Dutch Marsh his favourite fowling ground?' His question was directed more to himself than to his audience.

'It was. So it was. I ofttimes seen him there, coming back with a brace or two,' young Jack Ffinch interrupted excitedly. Others joined in.

'Or three …'

'Was good at his business calling, was Eph Woods.'

The churchwarden called to the landlord to replenish his mug. Such a long speech had to be underlined by liquid sustenance.

'That he was,' whistled old Bert Howard through missing teeth, 'though he did move around to wherever he fancied his luck. Quite successful, that's true. The Fothergill brothers weren't no match. No match at all.' The others nodded in agreement.

'The Fothergill brothers? Now they might have?'

'Well, it was their punt he was found in.'

'What are you sayin'? The Fothergills? The twins? No. Do you think?'

'Out of jealousy?'

'They never? They wouldn't be dumb enough to put him in their own punt to be found? Would they?'

The group of local men huddling together in the snug were full of the excitement of the latest developments in the case that had everyone on tenterhooks in and about the village on the edge of the marsh and for quite some miles around. A dead wildfowler who had been strangled, but found in someone else's punt on someone else's patch with a knife in him …

Theories abounded. Who had reason to kill Eph Woods? If there was a killer on the loose, who would be next? Was it safe to go anywhere near the marsh? Or anywhere? Suspicions were voiced or hinted at. If at all possible, people avoided the marshes after dark.

Young Jack Ffinch – though truth be told, it wasn't exactly his age that gave him the suffix 'young', just that he was the youngest in the group – by virtue of a strong-willed mother did not dare miss evening service or any other service in the little church on the mount. 'It wouldn't have been our parson who was friends with Eph Woods. Maybe the last one,' he said, '… certainly not this one. Not our Parson Sterk. You should have heard him ravin' about the iniquity of sin an' the floutin' of the Ten Commandments. Never seen him so livid. Makin' him late for service an' killin' people an' doing it with his knife. It was parson's knife stuck in Eph Wood's back, you know – well, at least one that came from the parsonage. Last seen at the hogroast, it was, when we celebrated the queen's birthday.' He lifted his mug in commemoration and as a salute to his own knowledge. 'Good old Queen Anne!'

The others joined in and a great deal of ribald comments followed and some red faces were reminded of the antics that had taken place at those festivities.

John Benton, the teacher and village scribe, showed his blistered hands. 'Haven't been able to hold a pen since ringing them damned bells all day … And my muscles …' His left hand stroked his right arm's shoulder by way of eliciting sympathy.

'You'll have to write with your feet then, in the funeral book …' Young Jack thought his quip was hilarious.

The churchwarden brought the meeting back to order. 'The cunstables will have to make a report to the quarter court, so what can they report?'

'Couldn't he just have drownded? Be so much less messy,' Thomas Bell suggested somewhat sheepishly, speaking out quietly what many were thinking privately.

The churchwarden looked at him sternly, shaking his head at the young barge hand, 'You're trying to get us into trouble?'

Thomas shrugged his shoulders: 'Just sayin'.'

Harry Snusher had been sitting quietly by the fire in the inglenook, not joining in the banter, but clasping his mug with an intensity that might crumple it. His face had taken on an ashen pallor. Someone noticed.

'Codsfish, Harry, you look like someone's trodden on your grave.'

'I … I saw him last night.' Harry Snusher spoke with barely a whisper. 'Eph Woods. Saw him as large as life walking out on the marsh. Thought I'd never tell anyone … but … I seen him.' He lifted his mug to his lips quickly as if washing away the memory would help.

The others took notice now with benign grins on their faces.

'How could you see Eph Woods last night if he's dead and b …?' Young Jack's voice faded before he had finished the sentence. He had spoken out without thinking, but it was on all their minds.

'I sore 'im, I tell you. Out on Dutch Marsh.'

'That's not where he was found. He was found on Hall Marsh, more of two miles away, so how could you …?' The churchwarden carpenter had his doubts, but he, too, went silent when he looked at the speaker.

Harry Snusher was not to be shaken in his story. He knew what he'd seen. 'An' used that knife, as you said … the parson's knife … at the carving … good, sharp knife it was, too.' Harry answered through clenched teeth.

'Of course! I'd forgotten. You did the carving … What happened? I mean, what happened to the knife?' the churchwarden joined in. 'How did it get to …'

'I dunno. I left it. Stuck in the carcass it was when I last remember it. You better ask the women.'

The women would have cleaned and tidied up and portioned out any leftovers between them.

'I remember now. I fell over you. You'd taken to sleep not far from the carving. By the old lime tree. About one o' the last things I do remember, cursing your legs as were stuck out for me to stumble on,' said Old Bert.

Then he added almost reluctantly. 'I did see summat, tho', but it weren't no Eph Woods. I saw a giant with a humpback on t' way home that night, staggering.'

'You were too drunk to have seen anything,' young Jack cut in.

'You were staggering?' added Harvey.

'I did, I tell ee. I seen a giant. Huge he was an' with a hunchback.'

'Where did you see the huge hunchback? With you in the ditch?' Young Jack wanted to know.

The small group laughed out loud.

'You must admit you weren't sober that night, Bert Howard,' said the churchwarden in order not to call the old man a liar to his face.

'I may have been a little … you know, but I was never too drunk to see what I seen. Maybe that giant was drunk, the way he stumbled and hurried.' Bert stuck to his story in spite of their laughter. 'I admit I was sittin' down at the time. Came from Dutch Marsh. Went to Hall Marsh. I seen 'im.'

That was it as far as he was concerned. He took a long draft from his slightly shaking mug and settled back on the bench defiantly. The others looked at each other, smirking more than smiling, raising eyebrows and shrugging shoulders – a silent conspiracy that would not hold the old man up to further ridicule. Old Bert was

known to overindulge on occasion and the hogroast had been just one of those occasions.

Suddenly, in the silence that followed, the door opened and accompanied by a cold gust of wind Sam Felgate almost fell into the room. He was as white as a sheet, his shoulders heaving for a lack of breath. His teeth chattered and he'd lost his hat. Before he started to speak he turned again and ensured the door was shut behind him. 'I seen 'im. I seen 'im, again.' He stumbled up to the bar, still mumbling, 'I seen 'im.'

'You've seen who?' asked the churchwarden.

'Eph Woods. I seen Eph Woods.'

'Eph Woods is dead. You found him on Hall Marsh. We buried him. You know,' he stabbed his clay pipe in his direction to press home his statement.

'I seen him jus' now, I tell 'e. Not at Hall, out on Dutch Marsh. 'e was dead alright, but 'e turned …' Sam Felgate grabbed the offered libation, but the landlord pulled it back out of his reach. 'You're allus thirsty. First the cash.'

Sam Felgate's eyes rolled in disbelief, before he collapsed on to the nearest seat.

The churchwarden scratched his head. 'Have you been at the Geneva again, Sam?'

'No. I seen … Eph Woods. Clear as I see you.' His breath rasped and his teeth kept chattering.

'Not you, too?' Harry Snusher raised his voice, seeking for confirmation. 'I've seen him at Dutch Marsh, too …' His voice faltered again. 'Walking, large as life.'

Harry beckoned to the landlord: 'Put it on my slate.'

Sam almost snatched the mug out of the landlord's hand and downed it in one long swallow. Then he visibly relaxed, though still pale and shaking. Harry Snusher received just a grateful nod for his kindness. Theirs was a kind of kinship. They both had seen the dead man walking.

'I was not going to mention it,' came the voice of John Benton, the teacher, in the ensuing pause, 'but if there are others … My wife came back from her sister's last night and she passed

Dutch Marsh and she saw Eph Woods. She's ill abed. Has not left the house since, it afrightened her so. I would not have said it for people to laugh, but if you too … perhaps she did see?'

The drinkers in the snug stayed silent. A serious note had crept into the conversation. This was different, so many people seeing the dead man walking at Dutch Marsh. What did it mean?

Suddenly there was an almighty crash in the next room. At the same time a curse and a yell tore across from the pump room that was more animal than human, followed by a desperate, 'Stay away! Leave me in peace! It's your own fault!'

There were yells and more strangled sounds, shuffles and noises that turned into words, 'Stop hounding me! Leave me be! I only wanted to scare you off.'

The drinkers in the snug got such a shock that they sat frozen for a moment. All that talk of Eph Woods' ghost meant they were already on edge as they rushed together to the connecting door, towards the noise.

They actually got stuck in the door momentarily, pressing together like sheep trying to avoid the snapping jaws of a dog. Only the first few got a glimpse of the blacksmith's large yet pathetic figure sagging against a wall, his fists outstretched as if to push away some unseen assailant, mouthing gibberish and repeating the words, 'You shouldn't have made fun of me. I couldn't help it. You shouldn't have laughed.'

A trestle table had been splintered and upturned. A bench had fallen backwards and a drinking mug smashed, marking where the large man had been sitting.

Now his hands flew to his head, pressing against his temples as if to shut out the sounds and his eyes were shut tight. Nobody had noticed him sitting quietly in the pump room of The Barge, brooding by himself. He had not been very civil of late and people were ignoring him. As the room had its own entrance, none of the guests in the snug had even noticed him as he sat listening in to their conversation, mumbling into his ale and shaking his head in his torment.

Now they couldn't help but notice him. They heard him, speaking still, as one by one they filed in, now themselves quiet. They listened to the rambling confession.

'You with your fancy tales of furrin' places and the things you'd seen and done and would go back to when the time came. And her with her airs and graces and me being a lowly blacksmith and not going places.' He took a deep breath that sounded more like a sigh. 'How you could have her at the beckoning of your little finger and ...' Again he covered his ears in his torment. 'If only you hadn't laughed at me. If only ...'

With his eyes still closed, he rose to his feet again, his arms stretched out in front of him, the flats of his hands pushing away some invisible assailant, shielding himself in his terror. 'Leave me alone! Leave me be!'

The blacksmith collapsed again in his corner and began to sob like a toddler. Then his eyes opened and stared unseeing into the distance. It took several of them to avoid the large man's fists, to wrestle him and hold him down and eventually overcome him and bind him with the harvest rope the landlord handed to them.

The blacksmith still rambled. 'His neck broke so easily. And now he keeps coming back. People say they have seen him, but not as often as I have. He hasn't left me alone. Go! Go away! Keep him away from me! Arrrrgh ...'

The churchwarden asked a question and the large man stared at him, or at least in the direction of the familiar voice as if he were waiting for some fog to clear, the red fog that had torn through him when a dead man had pressed his revenge. Finally he seemed to focus and more coherent words began to flow. 'I thought I had been seen walking with him to Dutch Marsh, that's why I put him on my back and dragged him to Hall Marsh instead. Dumped him in a punt there. But that's not my knife as was stuck in his back. I never used a knife. I only wanted to scare him. He shouldn't have laughed.' Later, when he was sober, he came like a lamb. Never once did he mention the name Eph Woods.

'Bert, you did see a giant with a hunchback,' the churchwarden offered by way of apology for doubting old man Howard.

'The blacksmith, with Eph Woods on his back, would probably look like that, stumbling in the moonlight.'

When the day came the large man went to the gallows quietly. Eph Woods had been avenged. His ghost was not seen from that day forward, but young ladies of a certain haughty bearing did report from time to time to having been followed by a large man. When they hurried away or seemed to be scared, the ghost instantly vanished into the shadows.

Eventually even that stopped. Some said it was after Salome Sterk died unmarried because nobody had been good enough for her. On her deathbed, the jilted maiden had finally confessed what had happened at Hall Marsh the morning after the hog roast feast so long ago. She had lost the knife as she hurried on her solitary way home to the parsonage late the evening before and had gone out again early to look for it. Having found it, she had wandered a little on the sea wall in the early light when she recognised the wildfowler in the punt on the marsh and it was then that she got the idea of revenge for leading her on and then rejecting her. Eph Woods had filled her head with all the beautiful places he had seen and where he would take her and she had finally surrendered her virginity, though afterwards he had reneged on his promises. So she had waded into the muddy briny and got her revenge, even though he had been dead already.

5

GREY LADY'S VENGEANCE

Without the moon the night was dark as sin. A smuggler's moon, favourable by its absence. Of course, it was planned that way. On moonlit nights a lookout on the Downs can get a fair view over the Thames and all the traffic that moves upon it when passing through its reflected silver beam. Then the heights of Leigh church or Hadleigh Castle are ideal vantage points to spy as far as the shores of Kent.

Now only the half dome of stars lent their familiarity to the local knowledge as the flat-bottom boat glided almost silently across the shallows. There was little wind. Just the creaking boat itself and the regular muffled splash of oars could be heard by the small company it transported – apart from the occasional suppressed curse.

When they spoke, their voices were gruff. Little more than curt whispers. No need to attract attention, not even among the locals who knew of their presence and bought the wares they carried so secretively under their seats. You never knew where a spyglass was pointed or when someone was desperate enough to pass on information that could be turned into cash by the authorities.

The tide was low and they had to use all their skills not to be stranded in the narrow convoluting rills of brackish water that meandered between the marshy islands of the Ray. When they reached the spot of their furtive quest – nothing more than a stake forced deep and securely into the slithery mud – they were gratefully relieved. It was an innocent enough object from wherever one might view it, close to and in line with the rotting hull of a broken-backed boat – a landmark reference to the stake's position.

A barn owl screeched as it flew past and its wing almost touched the tall leader's face when he stood up to make certain of their position. He'd heard and felt the owl more than seen it. 'Curse that bird ...' he spat out. 'This be the spot. Now tie 'em secure and let's be gone. These shallows put the fear o' the Devil in me.' Jack Gardner was a poor sailor really, though he would have cut the man who dared say that to his face.

They tied the casks, well secured with hemp ropes, as low as they could reach to that leaning stake knowing they would stay safely in place, even with the shifting tides. The rising water would completely hide their presence and they could be collected as soon as a buyer had been contacted and circumstances for their delivery were right.

It was the final run of the night for the tall Gardner, taking the small boat for the last stretch across the marshy wastes and shifting sandbanks outside the safety of Candy Island's dikes and walls. Their last task was to return the sloop to Bemfleet's Church Creek

where it would innocently lie among barges, hoys and other oyster dredgers on the Hard as it always did, conveniently close to most of their homes.

Will Layzell, the other half of the Layzell and Gardner partnership, had a cousin, twice removed, who had that very night arrived in Rochester from a run to Calais where he and his crew had delivered a catch of oysters. They had returned with a mixed cargo of brandy, 'baccy', tea and haberdashery. Much of that had been transferred on to the Bemfleet sloop on the blind side of the harbourmaster's house on the Medway, before it could be officially inspected in the morning.

Guided in by a signal from a spout lantern on Hadleigh Castle walls, Layzell and his men had unloaded most of the night's haul in Mill Creek at the site of the old watermill at the base of the Downs. Layzell's young son had been told to meet them with a couple of 'nags'.

The youngster was in no way suited for the rough and tumble his father enjoyed. He was a small and anxious boy, afraid of his own shadow, some said, but Layzell would have none of that. 'He'll have to be a man sometime,' he'd say, making few allowances, and he made the boy ride beside him through the nights, on errands or deliveries, to learn the ropes.

He liked to talk big, did 'Lucky Layzell', but even he was beginning to suspect the unsuitability of the youngster. 'He wants to learn to read an' write an' such. What good be that to him in a gale or against a Revenue man's barker? His brother, now, when he's old enough, he's of different mettle. He be better 'n me, you mark my word.'

Layzell carried a pistol at most times, not just to impress the men and enhance his image. This night he felt important. This night he carried two pistols in his waistband.

As for the boy, it is difficult to say, but he was more afraid of his father than anything else. Shivering with fatigue and fright, he led one of the laden horses from the overgrown remnants of the old mill in the lee of the 'hogback' hill around the castle hideout.

'You ain't been followed by no Revenue man, I hope?' growled his father, quite out of breath.

'No, I weren't, I went the long way round by Thundersley, honest.'

He wouldn't have admitted it, but his father was quite proud of him at that moment. Perhaps he'd make a man of the boy yet.

Some of the contraband was stealthily manhandled by two of the crew to their hiding place up in the vaults of the neglected, ivy-and-bramble-covered castle ruins. Coming up that way through the shrubs and malformed trees they could not easily be seen from the height above, nor silhouetted against the river. So skilful was their disguise and so secretive were their actions, that locals were convinced there had to be a tunnel up to the castle and maybe further up to the inns of Hadleigh village.

The two men were on edge, wary of every odd sound, every broken twig, anything that moved. Neither would mention it, but it was on both their minds – Hadleigh's Grey Lady. Those who had met her, if they were to be believed, were loath to go out after dark and the castle ruins were the scene of the more lurid encounters.

Both were breathing heavily under their loads, though they were lightly dressed after a hot day.

'What was that? Stop trying to scare me. I don't scare easy …'

The first of the two, Alexander Pye, dropped a half-anker and lashed out wildly behind him and to his side with his free hand.

'What's up wi' you?' enquired his companion, John Crozier, as he followed close behind and the barrel rolled against his shin. 'You tryin' to break my legs?'

'Not me, you!' shouted Alexander, feeling not a little foolish, but in his annoyance he had to take his anger out on somebody.

'You slapped my face. It's not funny, you oaf.'

John was a little short of breath from the exertions, but he managed to stutter, 'I'm three … four … steps behind yer … how can I … slap yer bloody face from down here in the dark … with both hands full?'

His co-conspirator turned around to land a punch with his free hand, but he stopped in his tracks when he realised even in the dim light that the silhouette behind him really had both his arms full and could not possibly have slapped him.

'Mayhap it was a branch,' he said resignedly. 'You stopped the barrel I dropped?'

'It's up against my leg. Nearly broke it.'

Alexander struggled back down and managed to pick up the dropped dead weight, before turning and struggling back up to the broken walls of the castle. They had to go down a second time to collect the rest of the smuggled goods, bundles of lace and packages of tea, bulky, but not nearly as weighty.

This time it was John who went first. It was about the same spot as before when he felt a distinct stinging slap against his face. Swinging around he hit out with several packets of tea in an oilskin. It slapped his companion against the side of his head and he lost his balance in the unexpected move. Stumbling backwards, Alexander fell headlong into a snaking growth of brambles that were not kind to his face.

'Serves you right for slapping me,' John said. He managed to free one hand by doubling up loads in the other and felt rather than saw his way the few steps back to the muffled curses that came from somewhere near the ground. He managed to pull his colleague back on to his feet before turning and rushing back up and out of harm's way. He could not see the scratched face in the poor light, but he knew better than to wait around. By the time his swearing companion arrived he had pulled aside the shock of brambles and ivy that were ideal for hiding their well-wrapped contraband and could be pushed back into place, looking innocent enough.

'Here,' he said to his stumbling companion, 'give me the packets. I'm standing in the brambles. I'll push them deep.'

Alexander did as he was told, biding his time, fists balled in his pockets to exact his revenge as soon as the task was done. He heard his intended adversary moving the tangled mass of greenery back over their hiding place. John was himself now cursing the thorny brambles and stinging nettles, when Alexander received another slap about his face, and another, unmistakably delivered with some expertise and force. He swung around, only to see the faint glow and outline of a lady in a long pale dress floating more than walking away and disappearing into the night.

He stood still as if nailed to the spot, his chin dropped, mouth open. His companion joined him, slowly and warily, but there was no need to be wary. There was no attack.

'Wha's up wi' you?' John asked. He got no answer, instead he heard a slow passing of breath that had been held too long.

'Did you see that?'

'Did I see what?'

'The ... there ...' Alexander pointed in the dark, a gesture that was lost on his companion. 'A woman! A woman slapped me ... A wo–?' He stopped himself from uttering what he was about to say. His hand fumbled about for somewhere to sit. He touched only nettles and growled at the stinging pain.

'A woman, you say?' Now John, too, whistled as he exhaled.

'The Grey Lady ...'

'You're playing me for a fool. The Grey Lady ... unless ...?' He realised it would explain his own experience.

'I seen her again. Why me? Allus me?' Alexander said it quietly and breathlessly, almost with awe. They had been in the presence of Hadleigh's Grey Lady and they couldn't tell, or else they would give away the secret of their stash.

Not so long ago that venue had served the infamous Gregory Gang for a similar purpose to theirs when one Richard Turpin was among their number. However, the Gregorys had moved on to fresh fields when it got too hot for them in the area, making room for Layzell and Gardner.

Some said the Grey Lady was a woman wronged by the Gregorys, come back to seek her revenge. Others argued for a former occupant of the castle who had been badly used by one of the king's knights and then been abandoned to her fate, finding suicide the only end to her shame. There were many theories.

Will Layzell believed never to keep all his ill-gotten goods in one basket. That's why they were split between the deep of the creek and the height of the castle dungeons, though this time there was a more devious and secret reason for that decision.

While Jack Gardner operated in the creek and two men hid more contraband at the castle ruins, Layzell and his reluctant son made for the wild reaches of Dawes Heath inland, to meet up with contacts, runners and merchants for immediate transactions. As one horse was laden to capacity, on this occasion the son was allowed to sit behind the father on the outward ride. On horseback the boy's deformity since birth, which had left one leg just slightly shorter than the other, was barely noticeable.

At the close of the hot day, clouds had begun to gather low on the horizon to the west. Distant thunder could be heard now and then and lightning, reflecting off unseen clouds, added an eerie dimension to the night.

The rendezvous on the heath was akin to a thieves' kitchen to the young Layzell, with shadowy figures inspecting goods, arguing, haggling. Deals were struck and money changed hands. Here and there, the odd flicker of a hurricane lamp added to the atmosphere momentarily by distorting sizes and shapes among the shrubs and low trees. Occasionally voices were raised and curses uttered under breaths that reeked of samples taken.

At the conclusion of the transactions, where the young Layzell looked after the horses and did his best to act grown up, Layzell Senior carried the fruits of the night's labours hidden about his person. Still he took no chances, following another route back to his smallholding close by the common in Bemfleet. Without his extramural activities, his place and plot were far too small to provide for the survival of his large family.

He was feeling pleased with himself. He would be known as 'Lucky Layzell' in future. All his wasted life he had been in scrapes and fights to be rid of the tag he had been saddled with from an early age – 'Lazy Layzell'. He'd show them …

They'd have to hurry, or daylight would overtake them. The child gingerly kept close to his father on the smaller horse. He could barely stay awake. But no sooner had they left the place of open-air commerce, in a cutting worn low by centuries of cart-wheels and hooves and without an easy escape to either side, than a figure as if from nowhere barred their way. Layzell did not see him until the horse shied suddenly, and it took both his hands to stay in the saddle: 'What the devil, fellow, get out of our way, or you will feel our pistols,' was his instant and ill-considered reaction.

'Not afore ye feel mine,' came the gruff reply. The interruption had been so sudden, the shadowy figure had taken the reins of Layzell's disturbed horse, pulled down the bit at the same time with a powerful arm, stretching the horse's neck downwards and causing the hapless Layzell to slide forward, almost losing his balance.

'Do something, man,' he shouted back over his shoulder to the boy.

Behind him the smaller horse, confused by the sudden stop and tussle in the dark, and without an experienced rider in charge, reared up and raced past the father and the stranger.

'That's right, get the constable,' was Layzell's face-saving shout after the disappearing lad. Leaning forward on the mane of his horse, he felt the cold muzzle of a pistol against his cheek.

'Don't be doin' anything to vex me now, friend. Jus' deliver your purse an' ye 'll live to tell the tale.' The voice was unhurried and confident, though somewhat muffled through the triangle of a protective kerchief. As if its owner had done this sort of thing a thousand times before.

Will Layzell tried to think fast. This close up, he could just about make out the outline of his opponent, but at that very instant a distant lightning flash spread enough brightness momentarily to illuminate a pockmarked face, or at least some of it, with glowing eyes on a tall, stocky body. It seemed vaguely familiar. Hadn't he seen it somewhere or sometime before? Those broad shoulders? He tried not to sound scared.

'You picked on the wrong man,' his voice came strangled, with a mixture of fury and helplessness. At least his son was safe and would not witness his disgrace. He was outclassed and he knew it. A sharp tug cut his belt and his purse and his pistols had gone before he had a chance to reach for them.

'That's all I carry, this be an ill night for bus'ness …' Even while he said it, a hand slid inside his topcoat, relieving him of another hidden pouch.

The stranger wasted little time and very few words. That made his impact all the more chilling. 'Now I believe ye …' he said deftly, slapping Layzell's nag on its rump with the pistol-hand at the same time as releasing its bridle. The snorting horse bolted forward, carrying its rider along. A hollow laugh rang in Layzell's ears and a shout that sounded something like, 'Nice doing bus'ness wi' ye.'

By the time Will Layzell reined in his horse, he knew it would be fruitless to turn around, even if he had still been in possession of his pistols. That villain had been much too professional to hang around and get caught out by the likes of him.

He cursed. The operation was lost. A whole night's labour. His and his men's profits handed to a phantom. How could he live that down? Where had he seen those glowing eyes before? And that voice seemed familiar. That earthy smell of someone living off or on the land. Or under it? That was it. It had to be.

No one else would have that strength. He'd been confronted by the Devil himself. Layzell went cold with the realisation, cold and almost sick. The Devil had taken his money, but he still had his horse. Those shining eyes. Ah, but he still had his horse. His horse? What use might the Devil have for a horse? Walking home would have been most disagreeable with the coins he had still hidden in his boots. In his boots ... He still had his horse and the money in his boots. He was convinced now – he'd out-witted the Devil.

Layzell made good time, hoping the Devil would not change his mind and come in pursuit. When he came close to Eastway, on the outskirts of the village, he heard a sound even before his eyes could make out the shape of the horse before him against the lightening sky and the river. His son, slumped on the grazing animal, cried helplessly. He barely moved as his father grabbed the reins. He was past caring.

'Forgive me,' he sighed, utterly miserable. 'I couldn't go for the constable, now, could I? My horse just went off ... I'm sorry ...' His wet breeches felt uncomfortable, too.

For once, he did not receive the outburst and punishment he had naturally expected. 'It's all right, son, it can't be helped. You couldn't have fought the Devil. That's who it was. He came from the earth and went back the same way. But I beat him. I held on to the horse and my boots ... Next time we'll be prepared. Next time we'll take a cross.'

Will Layzell was glad they would be home unseen, or so he hoped. A few raindrops fell from a solitary cloud and cooled down his temper. There was still the tea and brandy left in the castle vaults and those casks tied safely to a stake in a rill in the Ray ...

It was late morning by the time Jack Gardner arrived at Layzell's humble dwelling to discuss the night's business and to collect his share of the profits. The first inkling he had that all was not well was when Will's firstborn limped out of the place at some speed with his head down low and without acknowledging the visitor.

'Shot straight past me, he did, without so much as a by your leave,' Gardner was to tell the rest of the companions later. 'Thought summat' was wrong. The lad's usually more cordial.'

Layzell did not want to speak to him either, at least not about the events on the Heath. When Jack Gardner greeted him with a cheerful, 'Hello, Lucky!' he winced. He was drinking already and he offered a mug of warm beer to Gardner.

Layzell's wife, with a babe in arms and surrounded by children, was fretting and wringing her hands when he bawled at her to keep her brood quiet or leave the room. This was men's talk. Bus'ness. The wife dutifully withdrew to the back kitchen, taking the children with her.

'We've been robbed,' Layzell said at last, emphasising the 'we'.

'What you mean, we've been robbed? We can't have. You only went to the Heath for God's sakes. You're telling me false, aren't you? This be no matter for jestin'.'

Layzell was serious. 'There was several of 'em – jumped me in the cutting from out of nowhere. Brutal they was – and well armed, one a real giant. They had me off the horse and took everythin'. Everythin'. There was gun barrels in my face and knives in my ribs … an' they got my pistols, too.'

He made a face as if he'd just bitten into a crab apple, or a sloe berry before the first frost. A distasteful business. 'Had been a good night, too. Sold everythin'. Got a good price for the tea. Obadiah Shuttleworth was there in person. Promised him more next time. And then that … I'm glad to be alive, I tell ye.' He took another large swig from his mug on the well-carved table.

Jack Gardner closed his mouth very slowly. 'You're jesting. Tell me you're playin' me for a fool,' he repeated. 'I reckoned on that money.'

'I swear by my young un's. Ask the boy. I got him away afore they could harm him. He was lucky.'

Gardner jumped up, ready to use his fists, then checked himself. You couldn't hit a man in his own home. He was reluctant to believe the wily Will Layzell, but if the boy had been there … The boy would tell the truth.

'Ev'rythin', you say? Ev'rythin'?' He sat down again, scowling. 'Mayhaps you be gettin' too old for this?'

The implied threat was not lost on the partner. 'Well, there's still the stuff at the castle an' yourn in the marshes.'

'Oh, that be better, then.' Gardner nodded and scratched his head: 'I forgot the castle. But no thanks to you. We'd better keep a lookout then …'

Layzell agreed readily and shouted to his wife that they were going to the boat and the pair set off for the Hoy Inn on the water's edge to collect the rest of the crew. An idea passed through Will's scheming brain. Would it be possible, in view of the night's loss, to recover the contraband in the creek without arousing the crew's or Gardner's suspicion?

They were an odd couple: the tall, almost handsome Jack Gardner, with a shock of yellow hair inherited from his mother who came of Candy Island's Dutch stock; and the shorter, burly and balding Will Layzell. Both had been in trouble with constables and revenue riding officers on several occasions. Layzell had learnt the hard way to think before he acted and he played his cards close to his chest, trusting no one. Gardner had a hard and callous, almost destructive core to his nature that could be an asset if kept under control, but was also a constant worry to his partner.

The news of the night's disaster did not go down well with the men, but that sort of thing was to be expected occasionally in a trade such as theirs, when thief stole from thief and smugglers, too, were fair game.

'In future some of us will go with ye, not an unweaned boy,' said Gardner as they slipped out of Church Creek against the rising tide at first light. Layzell could hardly argue that.

'At least pretend you're dredging for oysters,' he urged the reluctant sailors who were quite content to slouch around, killing time while protecting their investment, sailing down to Hadleigh to keep the castle in view and back to the waters off Bemfleet. They were in the oyster channels, quite a legitimate occupation. That new ruling about not loitering at sea could not be applied here.

It looked so different from the few hours ago when some of them had been there last, so normal and not a bit as treacherous as it could be at night. Opportune seagulls followed them. Sheep were bleating on the low island to the south. They could hear curlews whistling plaintively across the saltmarshes and a cuckoo called from a thicket on the Downs, causing little Haggar Greenaway to suggest he hoped everybody had money in their pockets. He looked at Will Layzell when he said it. There was no answer, just a curse and a look that would have frozen a stranger; yet the peace was deceptive.

Gardner noticed it first. The russet sails of the revenue cutter came into view from the east, avoiding the Nore banks, then hugging the coast. They had developed remarkable skills, those government men, but then they were regularly paid, too.

'Someone ought to set fire to that damn customs house at Leigh,' Sam Jones said.

'Or scuttle their cutter,' added Haggar with a sideways grin, though he was the least violent of the five.

Will Layzell disappeared below and returned with a spyglass. Then placing it to his better eye, he screwed up the other one tightly, turning his face into a grimace. 'It be the cutter from Leigh alright, danged! They'll look the fools if they stop us.'

Gardner took the telescope from him to make doubly sure. 'It's that cursed Harrison among them. He being a Bemfleet man an' all. He ought to be stopp'd.'

'Do you want to be hanged for murder?' asked Layzell, trying to keep the thing in proportion.

Sam Jones fondled a handy cutlass and let the blade glide through his hand: 'I dunno, there ought to be a way.'

'I've tried making him an offer once, joking like, but he be incorr … incorr …' Layzell could not find the word he was looking for. He lied quite convincingly.

'Ungetattable?' offered Haggar Greenaway, keeping out of reach of his fists, just in case.

'Yeah, that be it. They pay 'em too much by half.'

'I hear it be near fifty pounds a year. One ought to be on their side.'

This time Layzell really let fly in his direction, missing him by a whisker. 'Know thee where thy bread is buttered, I hope.' Then he cursed again, as the feared and reviled cutter sailed past and into dangerous territory. Dangerous for the smugglers, that was.

'Curses on the crew,' mumbled Jack Gardner under his breath when the cutter hove to and someone scoured among the bladder wrack and kelp with a long grappling pole. 'They be getting much too close. If I find anyone has talked, I might well be hanged for murder.'

'No one here would nark, oi swear it.' The last member of the crew was quite reliable, if nobody made him an offer. You had to live in a place afterwards and that would not be easy. Looking after each other had sustained them through many generations as a community.

Layzell kept his head. 'Don't make it too obvious, watchin' 'em. They be thinking they be on a good'n if ye do.' They attempted to continue about their business, but it was difficult.

'Thank God the tide's high,' said Gardner, looking sideways where, out of the corner of his eye, he could see the revenue cutter getting much too close for comfort to the stake, which was thankfully almost invisible now. 'I swear they know somethin',' he said, scowling at each member of the crew in turn. They had all stopped what they were doing and watched.

The cutter was at the stake now. At high tide the specially designed boat could just about reach it. All eyes bulged as the grappling pole got stuck and through the spy glass Gardner could see several hands joining the two on the pole and first one, then the other casks were brought to the surface. The men stood in silence, unable to believe their eyes, seeing their hogsheads and half-ankers raised and lifted out of the water and on to the accursed government boat.

'May it sink with all hands!' Gardner spat out the words while checking the pistol in his belt, at the same time grabbing for a cutlass, which looked quite small in his hands. 'Shame you lost yours,' he indicated Will's empty belt. 'Let's go and sink the blaggards.' Sam Jones was prepared to join him.

'You sure you tied the goods secure and deep enough?' Layzell asked, trying to undermine Gardner's standing.

'They must have known summat, no way could they find that otherways. Unless …' Gardner looked about him again.

He met ruddy blank faces, except for Layzell, who tried to stay in charge: 'It's just a setback. We're still alright oursen'. Curse them. It's not worth losing your freedom for, nor the ship, not here in broad daylight. Better do another run. We've still got credit.'

He was right of course. Later the others were glad of his decision. That's why he was their leader. The hot-headed Gardner would get them into trouble soon enough. Gardner, too, slowly calmed down. The cutter had moved on and the revenue men were poking about another unlikely spot.

From the Downs the cuckoo could still be heard calling unperturbed and Gardner had to take his anger out on someone or something: 'That damn bird,' he growled through clenched teeth, 'if ever I lay my hand on 't, I …' he made as if to strangle something.

'You wouldn't know a cuckoo from an owl if you spied one,' said Haggar Greenaway from a safe distance, 'bet you turned many a man to a cuckold, though.' The others managed a knowing laugh, then settled back to accusing each other and bemoaning their luck. Being robbed twice within twenty-four hours was a crippling setback. Luckily their main stash at the castle remained intact.

It took several nights of wheeling and dealing and travelling for Layzell and Gardner to distribute the remaining goods. A small stone thrown up on a bedroom window to raise a sleepy customer, or sometimes a prearranged dropping-off place in a barn or hedge or hollow tree with a cash collection at a more public time, would settle an account. And, for a while at least, Jack Gardner would not let his partner out of sight.

Only the nearest and dearest – and not all of them – were told of the twin disasters that had befallen the smugglers, yet it did not take long before the news had spread all over the village and beyond, and taunts and needling remarks began to annoy the affected men. Sometimes it was just good old-fashioned banter and teasing, sometimes it was jealousy of past successes.

By the time they all met again in a corner of the Hoy tavern by the creek, next to the smithy on the churchyard, they were quite resigned that the best course was to ride it out and ignore the comments, though it was not always easy.

On a trestle table close to the hearth of the smoke-filled inn, William Matthews of Suttons Farm was in a melancholy mood. Surrounded by regulars, they had been discussing the latest smuggling tales and such talk always ended up with Matthews remembering his late father: 'My Pa, if he'd been jus' a little bit crooked, he could have owned Suttons instead o' renting it. He were as honest as the day was long, was my Pa. All the places he been, all the barges he sailed, there was many an opportunity for a bit o' skirt liftin' …'

'Oh, he weren't too opposed to that now, were he?' Robert Carpenter ventured a ribald comment.

'I don't mean that. You an' your foul mouth. I mean the bus'ness …'

'I know what you mean. Don't take on so. I still remember him, your dad, as if it were yesterday. But who wouldn't. Allus a friendly word for everyone, but I grant you that – he were honest, were your dad. I remember one time …'

He never got to tell his story. The grizzled beard of Jonah Whale, glistening damp with ale and saliva, separated, showing an odd assembly of yellowing teeth, as he noisily burst into a verse of his favourite sea shanty.

William Matthews raised his voice above the din: 'Still, there was allus enough bread on our table. Even for the many of us.'

'I lost count summat. How many of you are there now, what with all the fever an' that?' asked a tactless companion.

'We get by.' William evaded the question that was obviously a painful point to him. With five wives – 'Not all together, of course', he used to say – and some thirty-three children, his father indeed had been of extraordinary stamina and had been known the length and breadth of the Thames hereabouts. They had indeed been a large family, though many of his siblings had died in infancy and some had left home now to work and gone into service. Some were married and had moved away. And some had even been born away, if the truth be told. William Matthews was like a father to the remaining younger ones.

Sam Lemmons, village constable of the year, tried to cheer up the conversation and asked the landlord to refill their mugs: 'Rector Clerke must have taken a fancy to him to pay for that stone in the churchyard. That's summat to be proud on, that is, an' no mistake.'

'All this talk of honesty makes me thirsty. I bet old Matthews took his chances like anyone.'

'No, he never. My Da were with him sometime and he swore that John Matthews was the most honest man he knew. He were just unlucky with his women, them as dying of the fever and in childbirth an' such.'

On the corner table behind a sturdy oak beam, the smugglers were listening in.

'An' him allus picking lusty fertile wenches ...' Jack's eyes followed the buxom maid who had started more than working at the tavern – if the rumours were to be believed – though nobody could actually prove anything from experience or was prepared to own up to anything that could be said against her.

The wholesome and able wench had arrived on a barge and stayed behind to avoid a bad situation. They had soon found her indispensible at the Hoy. Her deft arms and sharp lashing tongue had become common knowledge – an asset to local folklore that mothers and wives suspected and men dreamed about.

'You ever met up with old man Matthews on your travels, Prudence?' Gardner asked the question without much finesse. It was just luck and Jonah Whale that prevented it being overheard by William Matthews. There might have been a fight early in the evening.

'You wash your mouth, Jack Gardner,' said she of the coveted features, 'speaking ill of the dead an' all. Mind what they say about you someday soon when you catch a revenue man's bullet. Who'll cry for ye then? And keep those roving hands to yoursen.' With a swirl of her skirts she sidestepped his grab.

'So what'll it be, Jack Gardner, or are ye thirsting for summat else ye are in the wrong place for?'

'I thought I found the right place,' was Jack's lame attempt at a joke. 'An' fill us all up on account of our bus'ness ...'

'Someone's been fishing for it, I hear,' came a remark from another table above the general noise, followed by a chorus of ribald laughter that refused to die down.

Gardner was up in a flash and with his hands about the struggling fellow's throat. 'What you been hearing, ha, tell me! Now! Tell me! You fishing for trouble, fellow?'

The young man choked. Will Layzell was beside him in an instant, prizing Gardner's hands away: 'How can he tell you anything with your hands on his windpipe? Come and sit down. Our mugs are full.'

'You're on a short fuse tonight,' said young Haggar, as the two partners returned to the table. He was still reeling from the sight of the wench's loose top as she bent low across the table to refill their cups. 'What a woman,' he sighed with a longing look. 'Jus' the woman to run a tavern with.'

Will Layzell meanwhile went to soothe the attacked fellow's ego by offering drinks all round. Then he had a quiet word with the landlord, taking orders for a future run to Rochester. They might make the trip to the Continent themselves once they'd made enough profit for a bigger cargo.

'I came by some strangers earlier with news from Maldon,' confided the landlord. 'Hear tell that John Vaughan of the Hall tried to claim certain merchandise as found in the Creek as shipwreck, him owning the rights an' all. "No way," says the revenue man, "them casks was tied to a stake. That's not shipwreck, that's contraband."' He laughed a hearty laugh. Then he added in passing: 'You were seen, though, close by, you an' Jack an' others. Better keep Jack on a leash.'

Layzell gave a nod of understanding to the landlord. He had already taken steps to curb Gardner's temper and ambitions. Referring to his lordship up at Jarvis Hall, he said: 'The devil, he tried to get hold of the goods without paying us, ha?'

'I thought some was meant for the Hall anyhow,' laughed the landlord, who found the whole episode quite hilarious.

'Have to put up our prices to Jarvis Hall.' Layzell, too, was beginning to see the funny side of it all and went back to the table to share the story with his friends. And order more rounds of cheap ale.

There was one notable absence among their ranks. Alexander Pye had not been seen since the night he and John Crozier had hauled their stash up to the castle ruins, but as his protective mother kept his movements under tight control, that was not unusual. John, too, had been quieter than usual.

Now Will Layzell commented, 'Alex been meeting the Grey Lady again, or has his mother found some other reason to keep him in? You're his best friend, John, is he ok?'

Crozier mumbled something inaudible and his face took on the colour of beetroot.

'You haven't seen him?' persisted Layzell.

'No, not since the night,' came the uneasy answer.

Young Crozier was strong and sturdy but a poor liar and Layzell sensed there was something amiss. In an emergency the boy's almost painful honesty might spell danger for the rest of them.

'Anything happened that night we ought to know about, John?' Layzell kept needling the red-faced young man.

Crozier remained silent.

'Between you two and the Grey Lady …' Layzell bit his lip, trying to stop himself speaking. The Grey Lady was a handy ploy to keep people away from the castle area.

'Grey Lady? Not you, too? Some people will believe the moon's made of Candy Island cheese.' Haggar felt big as he said it, but the next moment he was nursing a swollen lip. 'What …? What did I say? What's up wi' you? Anyone would think you've made her acquaintance … personally?' He emphasised the last word while pushing his head back to stop the flow of blood from his nose.

'It's no laughing matter,' stuttered John, nursing his knuckles, 'there really is a Grey Lady. Alex seen her an' she hit me, too.'

The conspirators were huddled with their heads together now, as this was a part of their 'bus'ness' that was good for not being seen, but if this went abroad people would ask why the two young men had been up there at night.

'What happened?' Layzell asked with a whisper.

Crozier's arms still bore the marks of the night's close contact with brambles.

'I'd rather not say,' came the stubborn reply. 'But she really frightened Alex. She really did. She's real alright.'

Layzell realised that Crozier was right, this was not the place to discuss such a delicate matter and he changed the subject with a rude comment about the much admired serving wench.

As their laughter filled the small tavern, Jonah Whale imparted more of the wisdom collected during a long life at sea: 'You throw your nets where the gannets dive … and drift with the nets … for a fine catch of herring …'

Even so, Layzell was expecting trouble, the way Gardner was drinking. Some folks get melancholy with drink and some get romantically inclined – with Gardner it was aggression. He felt like taking on anybody and the world and could be a danger to himself. Layzell had to get him out of there. The 'owlers' had another call to make …

'Jack,' he said urgently but quietly, as if he just remembered a forgotten errand, 'it's bus'ness. I jus' been reminded of an order we got to take at the Anchor. Don't like to go there alone. You better join me.'

Jack Gardner was reluctant to leave. He still hankered after Prudence Couch – for that was her name – and he had the devil in him that night. Still, there'd be ale at the Blue Anchor, too, and he was in the right frame of mind to stand his ground.

They left the smoke-filled, claustrophobic atmosphere of clay pipes and cheap ale under a low ceiling and turned uphill. Across the road, the Crown was a little less boisterous than the Hoy, but one could not miss the hearty laughter of Purkis the blacksmith, which echoed around the cluster of houses near the quay.

The Crown tavern was respectable enough for the vestry meeting of parishioners to adjourn to, its welcoming hearth fire and warming brandy paid for by the parish and supplied by Layzell and Gardner through the back door.

Small thatched houses and shops lined the churchyard, showing little light apart from the reflected glow of an open fire or an upstairs candle.

The shoe scraper beside the entrance door to the Blue Anchor came in useful even after the short walk up the narrow street. This was where the traveller stopped in past times on his pilgrimage to Canterbury, before cadging a ferry ride south across the Thames. Even now, the road to Candy Island passed right through the courtyard of the fine old timbered building, before turning east and then south over the common and downhill to the stepping-stones or the ferryman.

By comparison with the Hoy, the atmosphere at the imposing Blue Anchor was almost sedate, in spite of the company of young farmers and friends who were celebrating the impending nuptials of one of their number. Some acknowledged the late arrivals somewhat sheepishly – shopkeepers and craftsmen – the rest of them paid scant attention. Certainly Layzell and Gardner were not asked to join the celebrations.

John Brewitt, the landlord, rose from the table to take their order. Just for a short while he joined them, discussing his latest needs in the way of 'hot' brandy, Geneva and wine. Some of his customers had expensive tastes. 'My wife has need of some things in the shop, too, muslin an' calico, an' Dr Clerke likes his tea. But she'll see you herself.'

On another table some local yeomen and barge owners were talking business: John Loten and Lewes Bell discussed the possibility of joint operations and anchorage arrangements down on the Hard. The flamboyant Loten, whose brother Robert 'the Governor', was of international fame, and the dour Bell, son of Giles Bell of Thundersley Lodge, had a common bond in that just like Jack Gardner they were of Dutch stock from the now secured and walled island.

The subject under discussion was not the most edifying – the old problem of increasing the yield from their barges by making each journey pay – returning from London deliveries of wood, farm produce and hay with the horse manure of the London streets so useful to their fields.

Casually in passing, some of them stopped at the two smugglers' table to ensure a continuous supply of their special Geneva when next they got the opportunity. Even Gardner was beginning to feel like a businessman and, to be honest, he began to like the feeling and the importance that it implied.

Among the group of revellers, however, inebriated fortitude turned to needling and baiting comments. Sam James raised his voice to ensure he could be heard across the room: 'I hear Dick Turpin's been seen in these parts again those past days. I wonder what he be up to in this neck o' the woods?'

'Or who the lucky victims are this time? I never carries much about my person when I'm travelling, nor keep much at home, jus' in case.'

Did they know something? Will Layzell was inclined to think that the author of that last comment was someone who did not like to part with the 'filthy lucre' at any time for whatever reason, being a farmer, but wisely he kept his opinions to himself.

'There's someone who'll need a brace for a stretched neck one of these days,' laughed Thomas Barber, apothecary and surgeon, while his hands tied an imaginary noose.

James Waller, the church clerk, winced in his chair. He was in exalted company and he knew it. 'How is it that everybody knows that villain, but nobody has ever seen him? I never carry much about my person either, not like some of you gentlemen who travel so much. Not like you, Master Smith.'

The Peter Smith he addressed was the young churchwarden and the owner of some considerable inherited estate. 'Never had the pleasure,' said Peter Smith, 'though I wager he would have his troubles relieving me of my purse. And I lay odds that he's not as tall and mighty as people say he is. Only five foot nine, I'm sure. I wish I'd meet him when I've got my hounds with me.'

'I wish I was that confident, though I believe he travels on his own these days,' added Waller the scribbler.

Will Layzell had gone pale as a sheet as he listened. His lower lip began to tremble and he whispered to his partner, 'If it wasn't the Devil, it must a' been Turpin who stopped me in the lane …'

Gardner's fists balled until his knuckles shone white. He looked at Layzell, who shook his head as if to say 'let sleeping dogs lie'. Then he said with a broken voice from behind a shielding hand: 'We're only here for the bus'ness, remember?' It was hard for Gardner to see such good sense, but he tried.

Layzell tried hard too, to get a grip on himself. 'What do they know?' he added, 'I'd like to see young Smith meet the cutthroat. And he doesn't travel alone. I can vouch for that.'

He had encountered the highwayman years ago and he now remembered the eyes he'd seen while lightning lit up the cutting from the Heath just a few nights earlier, even if he'd embroidered the circumstances a little.

Gardner had given him the benefit of the doubt. His first instinct was to tell someone, brag about it: they had tussled with Dick Turpin. But Layzell had lost. No need to draw attention to themselves. Layzell nodded an emphatic 'no' and nudged Gardner, to remind him. Gardner bottled up his temper, scowling.

Around them the drinks flowed, toasts were drank and bawdy advice given to the would-be groom.

'They have no idea, do they?' Layzell felt out of place in such company. Gardner tried to drown his feelings of inadequacy while getting more and more irritated. 'They be drinking our brandy, but not wi' the likes of us.'

Somewhat reluctantly, at least in the case of Jack Gardner, the partners were about to make for the door when a commotion stopped them in their tracks, 'Gentlemen! Gentlemen! Have you not heard?' The landlord, moving between tables, had joined the group of well-to-do locals. 'Young Adam 's just come in with news. Dick Turpin, curse him, has been hanged up at York. The news has late come off the barges. I thought everyone knew. Swung like a pendulum, they say. Sounds like we can all rest assured in future … his robbin' days are over.'

The pair found themselves outside, where the fresh air revived them a little. 'Them an' their fine airs,' croaked Will Layzell, as they stood in the courtyard of the Blue Anchor moments later. 'Bloody cheese-makers and manure-merchants.' He was determined to get his own back. In the dark he could not see the anger in Gardner's face.

'You …!' In his anger, Gardner could not find his words. Instead his fist flew at Layzell. It glanced past the smaller man's nose.

'Now what have I done?' Layzell asked in surprise.

'You …! You told me Dick Turpin took our money. How could he, seeing he be up at York? You lied to me, you …' Words failed him again, but this time Layzell was waiting and dodged the fist, helped by the fact his eyes had got used to the dark.

'I told the truth. I know that pock-mark'd face anyways. That was Dick Turpin, on my children's heads. I know'd him and I seen him.'

Gardner was still seething, though even in his inebriated state he realised there was an edge to what his friend said that he recognised. Layzell seemed to be convinced. That did not alter the fact.

'You was robbed by a man who met the hangman hundreds of miles away, days ago.' He calmed down momentarily, proud of his deduction.

'It's as I tell you, Jack. I'd swear on the Bible.'

'But …'

The two men had started wandering away from the inn when Layzell suddenly grabbed Gardner's arm, like a drowning man, as the solution – what he saw as the truth – hit him.

Gardner tried to shake him off, then had to grab him when he saw the small shadowy figure beside him stumbling and sagging at the knees. 'You be awright? I never hit you …'

'No,' came the strangled answer, ' … don't you see? If Turpin was not here in person, it must 'a' been his ghost who …'

Gardner attempted to shake some sense into him, but to no avail.

'I did see him. I knowed him. Those staring eyes …'

The two men walked side by side, Layzell trying to come to terms with the fact he had been robbed by a ghost, Gardner not knowing what to believe. Eventually it was Layzell who spoke. 'If Dick Turpin is back, if only in spirit, an' he be that strong, I be looking forward to any o' *them* getting a feel of his pistols …' He felt better with that. After all, he had lived to tell the tale, but would those rich people they'd left behind at the Blue Anchor be that lucky?

Gardner was still trying to make up his mind.

'I've a hankerin' after pheasants,' Layzell said suddenly, changing the subject. 'I noticed a flock in Mad Bullock Thicket, up by Dean's Wood the other day. Would serve the duffers right. You game for a bird?'

Gardner did not have to think twice. 'You got the sulphur? Be my kind o' justice, that, when they're down here lording it.'

They had turned south through the thoroughfare and were walking on the common. 'Got to call home first,' said Layzell. 'You wait here, I'll be right back.'

❖ ❖ ❖

The night offered little light, though the sudden hushed voice from the shadows was familiar enough.

'Pssst! Jack? Jack! I've been waiting for you, Jack. It's late.' The soft voice was as urgent as it was pleading.

'It's not late, it's early. What the devil are you doing here, woman?' Gardner's voice was rough and forbidding.

'I thought you would be in the stocks or in the lock-up or something. I brought you breakfast.' They were in the vicinity of the noted village correction receptacles. Expecting Layzell's immediate return, Gardner roughly pushed the clinging woman aside.

'Don't need no breakfast yet. I'll be home when I'm good an' ready. This be men's bus'ness. Can't you understand?'

Gardner simply walked away, though the voice followed him with another plea. 'You come to me at night, why can't you love me in daylight?'

Her feet were muddy and the hems of her skirts felt damp as she slunk away.

It had not taken Layzell long to gather the necessary items from an outhouse. He had overheard enough of the conversation to give him an idea as to what was happening. He stayed away for a moment, then joined Gardner as he strode and stumbled up East Street, then up by the footpath and wood-fellers' track towards the Hadleigh plateau.

Layzell could not resist saying. 'I don't know what she sees in you. The way you treat that girl … you don't deserve her. Walking all the way from the island with the tide on the turn an' the steppin' stones slippery. An' not even daylight yet. Why don't you settle down with her?' Layzell had fancied the besotted girl himself once, but she would not give anyone else the time of day. No one else but Jack Gardner existed for her.

Now she'd return to a day of drudgery on the farm where her worth was scarcely appreciated. She stayed on in spite of the danger of the marsh fever, which struck down so many. With what she earned, she would ill afford Thomas Barber's medicine.

Gardner was unrepentant. 'Hah! She be good for a tumble in the hay, but I'm not the marrying kind. Besides, I'd rather lie with Prudence Couch.'

Layzell was silent for once. He, too, was thinking of Prudence Couch and those soft cushions of hers.

Dogs barked at the Hall, still awaiting their master. When they approached the woods, a farmer came out of his cottage, carrying a storm lantern, with a dog at hand. For an instant they could see the dim light of the interior as the door opened and shut. Instinctively they had approached downwind. Now they pressed themselves into the freshly ploughed furrows of the field, face down, merging with the earth. Another sobering experience.

They were lucky. The soil was damp after a short shower and the dog did not pick up their scent. Man and dog at first walked some way towards them, taking the air following the disturbance. After a short while which seemed forever, the man turned and reversed his steps. The dog followed.

'For a moment then I thought we were goners. Maybe I *am* getting too old for this,' wheezed Will Layzell amid a string of curses, stroking the worst of the soil off his garments.

'Maybe you are,' agreed his companion in a way that confirmed Layzell's suspicion that he'd like to take over the operations. Layzell was convinced he'd have to keep the younger man and his temper in his place. That's why he had slipped a badly scribbled note to his one-time childhood friend Harrison in church last Sunday, while scowling at him with outward and unmistakable animosity.

The note had contained a simple message: 'Ten yards east Mary Bell Tuesday.' That had been enough to bring out the revenue cutter to the old wreck once called the *Mary Bell* and undermine Jack Gardner's standing. As for the revenue officer, he had an understanding with Layzell that suited both of them. Layzell would supply the odd titbit of information to favour the revenue in return for a blind eye on most of their operations. This way everybody won, but if Gardner had been privy to such information, he'd have murdered his partner there and then.

They entered Mad Bullock Thicket as quietly as their condition would allow. It did not take them long to ascertain the pheasants' roost. With a small tobacco tin fixed to the very top of a long, slender pole, they lit a piece of brimstone card, placed it in the tin and then closed the lid, which had been prepared with numerous small holes, thus enabling release of the deadly sulphur fumes. Raising the pole, the smoking contents at its apex hovered just a foot or so beneath a sleeping bird. Within moments it silently toppled dead off its perch into waiting arms. Two more birds followed before Gardner trod on a snapping branch as he lost his balance and a flurry of suddenly wide-awake birds lifted from their roosting branches in noisy confusion.

Instantly another commotion came from the house with barking dogs followed by opening doors. That caused them to pull the nailed tin off the top, stomping it into the damp ground and pushing the pole lengthwise into a convenient hedge before hurriedly departing downwind, clutching their catch under their jerkins as they vanished into the night.

No sooner were they safely out of harm's way when it occurred to Gardner that he was carrying just the one bird, yet his friend had two.

'Wait up,' he said to his partner in crime. 'How's it allerways come about that I ever gets the one while thou gets the two? Anyone would think that yourn better than me.'

'Well, it was my idea,' said the smaller man, 'an' my family is larger.'

'Yeah, but I did the handlin', an' that makes me the more deserving,' Gardner insisted. In a sudden fit of temper, Layzell hit him with one of the birds, a little harder than he had intended.

'Here ye are, take that if ye must.'

Not to be outdone, Gardner hit back, sending the smaller man flying out of reach. It was at that moment that he himself was slapped about the face with some force, and again as he straightened himself up and tried to focus. He should have realised it could not be the smaller Layzell, who would punch or kick but never slap; it just wasn't manly, but Gardner never did stop to think when the blood rushed to his temples and the red mist clouded his sight. Wildly he advanced, cursing, only to be slapped again, even harder.

His adversary wouldn't stand still, nor was there any kind of contact when he thought he had been close enough to hit back. It was too frustrating. But then he noticed that it was freezing cold and with that realisation came an inexplicable sense of dread.

He stopped flailing for a moment. His arms dropped to his sides and while he tried to focus on where to place his punches he was slapped some more. Now an angry female voice scolded him. 'Revenge at last! Call yourself a man? I've been searching for you, Jedediah. Oh, how I searched. So many men ... So many men ... Now I shall be free. At last I am free! You should suffer the way I did, but death is too easy for one like you. Oblivion while alive is all you deserve, you mean debouched rapist! You murderer of your own child! You beast!'

She followed those last words with an awful shriek that penetrated and destroyed Gardner's shallow mind as it contained the pent-up hate of centuries. Once more she slapped his face, laughing, as he stood there, shaking and mouthing gibberish, staring, but not seeing into her dark, hateful eyes.

With that the elegant pale grey figure of a woman – in a long gown like a nightgown perhaps? – floated away and dissolved into the early morning mist as the first hint of the approaching dawn began to brighten the sky to the east.

Will Layzell knelt on the dew-fresh heath, shivering, hands joined in prayer for his soul, as he thought he might be next, then staring at his companion with awe-struck intensity. He had never seen Gardner in such a state, half upright, half crestfallen, but silent.

Now he jumped up. 'Jack, what happened? Who …?' He quickly corrected himself: 'What was that? Jack! Jack? Speak to me, Jack! I only hit you with a pheasant. Jack? What did she say? What did she mean?'

Layzell had heard the awful words that had mistaken his business partner for some long-dead villain, but he had not understood. All he had seen was an indistinct ghost-like figure of an avenging angel who flew at Jack Gardner with a demonic intensity, or as he later explained it, 'A raging demon in the shape of a female, huge and awful and mad …'

At Suttons Farm a light came on and the dogs made a rumpus. Will Layzell supported Jack Gardner as best he could and dragged him towards his home. Jack babbled, struggled and stumbled, but there was no fight left in him. He was a changed man. Even the apothecary, when sent for, knew of no way to help him.

Layzell sent word to Gardner's father at Candy Island Farm and the young woman came and collected him on a high-wheeled cart. He would be all hers now, though not the way she had imagined. Jack Gardner never spoke again.

It wasn't until full daylight that some of the Matthews children ran out on to the Downs with their dogs to where they thought the sounds had come from.

'Look, the dog's found sum'thin',' one of the boys called out. It was a miracle. Three plump pheasants had dropped dead from the sky.

'Finders keepers, finders keepers …' exulted the boys grinning and big brother William concurred. Even for a family the size of the Matthews of Suttons Farm they'd provide a veritable feast.

And Will Layzell? Well, once he had recovered sufficiently from witnessing Jack's ghostly visitation, he was planning their next bit of bus'ness as the undisputed leader. After all, the revenue man owed him something now, didn't he?

Hadleigh's Grey Lady was never seen again.

6

THE VIKING ECLIPSE

A shadow spread over the land.

'Yes, this is it. This is the place where it happened. Here the Battle of Maldon was fought. Here and in the field back there, over the sea wall. That was in the year of Our Lord Anno Domini 991.

'This is where the waters "locked" as they still do on Panta's stream whenever the tide returns and the causeway disappears. And over there, that's where the sea wolves put up camp with their ships close by. On that island those Vikings felt safe. Ninety-three dragon ships, that was a frightening sight.'

He said 'was' like someone who had been there, Matthew noted with a curious grin. Together with his friend Graham and their young sons, Theo and William, they had wandered the mile or so along the sea wall from Maldon on a fine sunny day, intending to witness a rare natural event in a special place: a solar eclipse. They'd passed what looked like a ships' graveyard in a small bay, where barges and boats had been left to rot. Sometimes only the grim ribs like the ribcages of dinosaurs still rose from the mud.

'I remember a story from my childhood days about an elephants' graveyard somewhere in Africa where old elephants went to die. Probably just a story, but this reminds me somehow,' Graham had said wistfully in passing. 'What is this special place you are taking us to?'

'An ancient battle site. You may remember the story?'

Seagulls cried and curlews whistled and black-and-white ducks shovelled along the waterline around the grey-green tussocks covered by vegetation that rose from the rippling waves like small islands. Russet sails of spritsail barges spiked the horizon.

On arrival at the spot opposite the island they'd passed through a kissing gate where a rough road crossed over the sea wall. They had followed that road down to the water's edge, where some people had gathered already and they listened ardently to what appeared to be a historian or a guide, a small seedy man who looked more like a monk in sandals than a twenty-first-century citizen. He was obviously an interesting speaker, judging by the close attention the handful of people paid him, so Graham and Matthew stopped and tried to encourage the boys to listen also.

At first the youngsters were more interested in skipping stones across the water's surface once they got down to where the road vanishes into the waves, but they came to listen eventually, as the curious little man continued his talk: 'And on this side, some-where hereabouts, stood the Saxons who wanted to stop those raiders in their tracks, protecting their homes and their kin, and Maldon and its royal mint. There were wealthy traders in Maldon then. Maldon was one of the burh – or fortified – towns in this shire, just like Colchester and Witham. An important place to defend.'

'Corrr,' said Thed, 'they were making money in Maldon?'

The little man stretched out his arm, which was lengthened by his walking stick like a shepherd's crook and made a wide arc about the land and over the sea wall behind them: 'There was woodland all about here.'

Then he pointed to a particular area. 'Here Byrhtnoth arranged his men, advised and encouraged them, before he, too, dismounted among his loyal followers and sent back the horses.

'From the bank over there a messenger shouted across the Viking's demands: "Pay for protection and avoid the massacre. There is no need for us to kill each other if you are rich enough to pay us tribute. You can have peace for gold."

'"Peace for gold?" Byrhtnoth would not take the coward's way, instead he offered them spears as tribute and death from well-tried swords. He and his people would defend their homeland, Æthelred's kingdom: "You will not gain treasure so easily," he shouted back. "Spear and sword will decide who pays."

'And he ordered his men to take up their shields and stand on this bank of the river, two armies facing each other across the water, the Essex vanguard and the raiders from the ships.'

The boys looked at each other at the strange turn of the speaker's phrases and smiled, but stayed silent.

'Of course, the water was narrower then. The land was five feet higher then than now, so it was less of a distance when the two armies shouted and taunted each other, drumming swords on shields, wielding spears, each trying to intimidate the other side. Only arrows could reach and kill at that distance.'

The small crowd listened ardently; especially the children, who were hanging on every word. He certainly seemed to know his history, but some of his words were odd and some of the phrases sounded strange.

Theo and William were shadow-fighting with imaginary swords.

'He called it "Panta's stream",' commented Graham out of earshot, 'but surely it's the Blackwater?'

'Ah, yes,' said Matthew, 'but it's still called the Pant further upriver.'

'I didn't know that,' admitted Graham, 'and when the waters lock, I suppose that is when the tide closes in over the causeway? Years ago we read the old poem about the Battle of Maldon in school. It's a long time ago, though, but I have always wondered … It's certainly not difficult to imagine a horde of weather-beaten Vikings on the opposite bank and up that rise to the higher ground, baying for blood.'

'Who was Byrhtnoth and how did he get here at the right time?' one of the group wanted to know.

'The great ealdorman followed the call and the king, *rex Anglorum*, and he collected his army and moved south to meet the enemy, the scourge of the land. Those Vikings had already plundered Folkestone, Sandwich and Ipswich before they came to Maldon.

'At Ramsey Abbey our men were turned away, the abbot offering to only supply provisions for the ealdorman and seven men, choosing to ignore the multitude of warriors. Byrhtnoth's reply was as decisive as his sword arm: "The lord abbot knows that I will not dine alone without the men, as I do not seek to fight alone without them."

'So they came to Ely instead and were welcomed. Ramsey Abbey came to regret their lack of hospitality when Earl Byrhtnoth rewarded Ely Abbey with a very generous gift of lands.'

Again Graham asked Matthew, 'How does he know all that? Anyone would think he had been there. Strange. You certainly picked a good spot to experience the eclipse.'

In the wide-open space on the edge of the water, it seemed to get darker and an odd stillness crept over the land.

'Dramatic place for a dramatic occasion,' was Matthew's proud answer. 'A solar eclipse doesn't happen in everyone's lifetime. And we're lucky. The clouds should not interfere with the viewing.'

He brought out his specially purchased solar eclipse spectacles and put them on to shade his eyes when he looked directly at the sun, before handing them to Graham.

'I, me, what about us?' clamoured the boys. Before he handed the glasses to them, Graham made them promise never to look directly into the sun with their unprotected eyes. They would go blind, he warned them.

'Well, it's too bright anyway,' said William. Graham handed the glasses to Matthew's son, Theo, first. 'Remember that, or you may lose your eyesight.'

'Corr,' was all young Theo could say, 'the moon has taken a bite out of the sun.'

Immediately William reached for the glasses and tried them on. There were lots of 'oooh's and 'aaah's as the glasses went back and forth between the boys, who could barely conceal their excitement.

Among the huddled crowd the little man continued unabated, 'Well, the ealdorman Byrhtnoth, he was rich and of noble stock and very important in the country. And he looked it, too. An imposing figure, tall of stature, taller than the others, richly dressed and with long flowing hair – an easy target for his enemies, though he stood his ground heroically.

'And loyalty? Well, that he had in abundance. Nobles had pledged him their swords and their strength from as far afield as Bedfordshire, Huntingdonshire, Cambridgeshire, Suffolk and north Essex. It was Byrhtnoth's pride that was his downfall, a curse that has blighted many a great warrior. He allowed those wolves of slaughter to cross over the causeway, where three archers could have kept them at bay. Instead he ordered his men to form the shield wall and keep steady in their fight as the raiders stormed towards them. The roar of battle then thundered into the sky, where birds of carrion circled. Spears flew from fists and arrows from bows, piercing ringmail and body armour with sickening thuds. Shields were assaulted by the harrowing blows of spear, sword and seaxe, splintering the linden wood. The screams of the wounded and dying rang out. On either side young men fell dead, cut to pieces and eagerly the others vied in the killing.'

The light was definitely dimming now and people held darkened glass up to the sky to view the sun, which lost its power as the moon's circular shape crept over its surface. One enterprising

fellow had brought a piece of cardboard with a pinhole through which the light of the sun fell on to a sheet of paper. The shape it made on the paper was an ever-slimmer sickle.

'Byrhtnoth encouraged his men before he himself became the target, savagely gored by a spear that was broken by a shield. Still he stabbed at the attacker and his lance passed through the Viking's neck. Then another advanced. One of his squires, no more than a boy, pulled out the spear from his lord's chest, turned it and killed the attacker.'

Theo stabbed at William with the glasses and in the spirit of the story William fell down and lay still, feigning death, before he got up again and it was Theo's turn to theatrically die.

'Hopefully they'll never have to experience the real thing,' whispered Graham, as the teller continued.

'But the onslaught was relentless. More Vikings approached, armed and greedy for the earl's possessions. Byrhtnoth drew his ornamented sword. One of the seamen cut his arm and he dropped the golden-hilted weapon, no longer able to hold it. Still he encouraged the others and while saying his prayers, those fiends cut him down, together with Ælfnoth and Wulfmær by his side.

'When they saw the earl slain some of his men fled from the scene, the sons of Odda, Godric, Godwine and Godwig took to the woods. The cowards. One even took the ealdorman's steed in his hurry to get away.'

The teller of the story seemed to hurry himself now, as if there was not enough time to finish his account of the battle before darkness engulfed them.

'Others pressed forward instead,' he called out, gesticulating wildly. 'Young Ælfric and Ælfwine and Leofsunu resolved to stand firm and advanced though their lord was dead. Dunnere and Æscferth, the son of Ecglaf, fired their arrows, tore into enemy fighters; Edward the Tall and Æthelric rushed into the melee and killed many a foe. Offa the sailor was cut to pieces. Wistan, son of Thurstan, killed three before he fell. Brothers Oswold and Eadwold fought on, as did Byrhtwold, who raised his shield, shook his spear and exhorted the men to keep heart with their fallen leader. Yet another Godric fought with might and Æthelgar dealt out blow after blow until he himself was hewn down.'

The storyteller barely stopped for breath now. 'Terrible was the cost in lives on both sides, but still in the grip of bloodlust the victors robbed and plundered the dead and were offered gold by the king to leave these shores. A battleaxe or a two-handed sword severed Byrhtnoth's neck. They took our lord's head as a cheap trophy and carried it before them in victory back to the land of the Danes, together with their ill-gotten gold.'

While they'd been listening, sky, land and water had darkened. Night was falling in the middle of the day.

A shadow crept over the earth as the moon moved between earth and sun on its trajectory. To onlookers it was frightening, as the dark orb invaded the surface of the sun like some dark round beast devouring and taking a large chunk out of the provider of light. People talked in hushed tones, while watching the phenomenon. Children pressed close to their mothers and fathers, holding hands.

The speaker's words came quieter now, solemn almost. 'A darkness spread over the land. We carried the ealdorman's body back to

Ely and gave that beloved man a burial with honour. We placed a ball of wax where the head should have been …'

He shook his head as in shame or despair at the enormity of the disaster.

The dark and ominous silence felt like an eternity, and people were suddenly more conscious of their surroundings than usual, for once actually being able to look at the sun, but instead seeing the moon. Some of the smaller children were shushed by their mothers and others held each other rather tighter than necessary.

The two friends tried to pat their son's shoulders assuredly and press them close, but both boys shook off the familiar protection like the fearless men they were aiming to be.

A small dog whimpered and its owner picked it up and cradled it. There was no other noise apart from the hushed ripples of the water lapping the shore. No animal sounds. No bird calls. All was silence in the eerie twilight as the light failed and a strange darkness covered the land like a dark blanket.

Venus and other planets, the brightest stars, became visible in that darkened sky in the middle of the day. When the last sliver of the sun was covered by the moon, the sun's corona surrounded it like a beautiful gossamer halo. This lasted for some moments, when, like a diamond ring sparkling, the rim flamed into an intense white light – Bailey's Beads – when the sun's beams pass the deep valleys on the rim of the moon. A beautiful and unforgettable sight.

Graham turned to Matthew and whispered, 'Really one of the most awe-inspiring spectacles in all of nature.'

Again he felt for his son's hand to be close to him and make sure he appreciated the miracle up there in space, the rare if natural spectacle that would have disturbed people in past eons. People who could not explain what was happening would have fallen to their knees and prayed to their Gods and made offerings, begging for the return of the sun as the victor, as it was now, as a sliver of light returned with the moon's passing.

But Graham's hand could not find his son by his side. He looked down. William wasn't there, 'William! William where are you?' People shushed him as he broke the spell with his panicking shout.

His son was not to be seen. Where was he? Where was the boy? Matthew was alerted now too. Theo was missing also. Both boys had vanished.

In the slowly improving light, the two men looked at each other in panic. There was nowhere to hide. In the small crowd, people were holding the hands of their children. Some cradled the smaller ones in their arms. William was not among them. Nor was Theo. Light was returning, as the penumbra of the moon passed over the land.

Matthew ran back up to the sea wall for a better view from this vantage point. With a sigh of relief, he beckoned Graham to join him.

Beyond the wall, the boys stood close to a single tree by a small patch of greenery, backed by a semi-circle of shrubs and wild roses that glowed in the eerie light. A bank and ditch surrounded that small area, possibly to act as drain. Once all that would have been open land backed by woods.

The land where the battle raged?

The boys stood there, staring at something on the green patch of land, except that there was nothing there. They seemed to be in conversation with their invisible subject of attention.

A puzzling scene, though there was obviously no danger and the two fathers walked down to join them.

'William, what are you doing? Who are you speaking to? There's nobody there.'

'Theo, you're missing the eclipse. You may not likely ever see one again.'

'It's this poor man,' said Theo, 'he's lost his head and he keeps saying he's sorry.'

'What are you talking about, son? There's nobody there.'

'Can't you see him, Dad? He's very sad. He's covered in mud and blood and he keeps beating his chest.'

'But he hasn't got a head,' added William seriously. It did not occur to them to question where the sounds came from. As far as they were concerned the figure just stood there, utterly self-absorbed and unconcerned by its surroundings, except that the place was obviously what had brought him here.

'He is very large,' said Theo, 'or he would be if he had a head.'

'What man?' asked Matthew. 'What head? Are you two playing games again?'

'No, look, he keeps pointing at the island and he has been hurt. Maybe that was when he lost his head? He looks big. And he wears funny clothes.'

'What man? What clothes? There is nobody there.'

'Can't you see him, Dad? Can't you hear him? He's got a sword and a shield and he points to the island.'

'I'm worried about him,' Graham said to Matthew, who found it all very amusing. 'But if your son sees it as well … It must be because of the story of the battle that man told earlier.'

'The boys are having a game, can't you see?' said Matthew. 'Too many computer games and films if you ask me, but didn't we play at Saxons and Vikings when we were their age? I remember myself with an old pot on my head and a stake of wood rescued from a picket fence for a sword. The boys are no different, really.'

'Yes, but look at them. That doesn't look like play-acting to me. They really seem to be in conversation with someone.'

'I think he's sorry,' said William, 'He keeps on asking why he had to act so rash and so proud? Why did he allow them to come over the causeway? He must mean the Vikings, Dad.'

Suddenly the boys turned and hid behind their fathers: 'He is screaming now,' said William, 'he calls out names and curses the sea wolves.'

'Olaf and his sea wolves …' said Theo.

Matthew had seen and heard quite enough. He had to put an end to their charade.

'Can't you see him, Dad?'

'Can't you hear him?' Both boys turned to their fathers.

Matthew tried to be reasonable and adult about it. His son had a rich imagination, but they must have conspired to play out the story. That had to be the reason for their actions. He did not consider then that to hatch out a story to play a joke on the grown-ups, they would have had to sneak off at the height of the darkness during the solar eclipse.

'I don't see anybody. There is no one there,' said Matthew in desperation, throwing a knowing wink in Graham's direction that said 'they're playing a game'.

The boys were not to be shaken, 'Can't you see him? He is so sad. And he hasn't got a head.'

'Without a head, how can he speak?' Matthew expected the two boys to break out in laughter at any moment, when they

thought their ruse had worked and they'd hoodwinked the elders. To underline his superiority he walked in the direction the boys had been looking, determined to call their bluff. He did not get far when he suddenly stopped.

He started shivering. His teeth chattered. Quickly he stepped back from the spot he had invaded, 'Damn, it's cold there. That can't be. How can it be so cold just a few metres away? It's not poss ...' He stopped himself. How could he deny a fact? He was still shivering.

'Come on,' he said instead, 'let's go back to civilisation. The solar eclipse is over, anyway.'

The light had returned. The moon had passed the sun and bird-song and the cry of the gulls could be heard again.

'Maybe that's where he died, that fellow Byrth ... – strange name – maybe that's where he was hewn down and lost his head?' Graham wondered.

'Byrhtnoth? Could be. Then why did the boys see him and not we?'

'Children may be more receptive to restless spirits than adults? Who knows? Perhaps we were just not privileged?' Graham was prepared to acknowledge that maybe the boys had not been playing out a game. They were walking quietly now and not as boisterous as before.

'Wait 'til I tell them in school,' was all William said, 'they'll never believe me.'

Back on the sea wall, people were talking again and dispersing and some had started to walk back towards Maldon. The story-teller had gone.

'Where is the historian with all that knowledge of the battle?' Graham asked one of the audience in passing when he could not see the mysterious little man.

'Don't know,' was the answer. 'No one saw him leave. Seems to have disappeared into thin air during the eclipse. What an experi-ence. Well, I don't think I will ever see that again in my lifetime.'

A faint dark curve became visible under the water, between main-land and island, a curve that got stronger and turned out to be the causeway as the tide fell and the waters 'unlocked' and separated again, making dry-foot passage to – or from – Northey Island possible.

HISTORICAL NOTE

On Friday, 22 April 1715, the Reverend Roberts wrote in his church register:

> There was a total eclipse of the Sun between the hours of nine and tenn [sic] in the Morning and visible here in South Benfleet when that glorious Luminary was obscured, and it was observed to be extream [sic] cold, and several Stars appeared for some Minutes.

South Benfleet was the site of a bloody battle in AD 893 or 894, when King Alfred the Great's son and son-in-law with their armies routed Haesten, known as Haesten the Black, the Viking army, and cleared out their camp there with great loss of life and ships in this Battle of Benfleet.

7

ODIN'S
STORM

'EVEN MEMORY WILL DIE'

The long house seemed to be alive and in agony. Cattle were restless. Beams creaked. Shutters rattled. Was someone trying to gain entry? Was he not alone? Sighs and groans filled the ground. The old man knew it was only the wind, howling about the damp wood, whispering in the reeds above him, chiming in the rafters, tearing and pushing at the mud-plastered walls to gain entry. Or was it something more sinister?

The sounds would have been worrying enough, had he not been familiar with them since childhood. He shivered. The fire needed replenishing. As he was the only one at home he'd have to stir himself – not an easy task with the stiffness in his bones and with the wind blowing down like this. Smoke curled in the roof space above him among the dried fish, the sides of pork and venison and the bundles of sausages.

There was another sound, louder than the wind. It was determined rattling, like a cudgel battering the main entrance to the dwelling …

Wulfgar shivered in his greatcoat and went to throw open the inside latch.

'Who seeks to gain entry?' He shouted the bad-tempered words into the wind as soon as the door opened wide enough.

He took a short intake of breath when he looked up to a tall imposing figure shrouded in a deep black cloak. The biting wind tore at an unkempt beard, but much of the face was hidden by a wide-brimmed hat, revealing just one keen eye. An ancient spear in a bony hand served as a wandering staff. Strangest of all was the raven resting on his shoulder, with another one squatting close by on a branch of the linden tree.

Wulfgar pulled the warming garment tighter about his chest. His mouth had not closed with the surprise and the rude remarks he had been about to repeat failed him. Words failed him altogether. He was confused. One minute he had been trying to doze by the fireside, waiting for his sons to return from the hunt and his daughters from visiting their kinfolk in the neighbourhood, the next he was confronted by a most unexpected stranger.

Finally it was up to the stranger to break the silence. 'I hoped I might find shelter here from the wind, at least for a while? Would you offer a stranger your hospitality?' The voice was both familiar and yet totally strange. It certainly was not a local voice.

'So sorry,' the old man at last heard himself speak. 'Where are my manners? Please enter, stranger. You must take me as you find me ... for once I am alone.'

As if he had anticipated the words, the stranger stepped past the old man into the large open interior that would normally be teaming with the people and servants of the household. There were all the signs of wealth one would expect of a leader of men. A man of power and standing with his own four-legged standard close by the fire and his favourite seat. Bowls and tubs and buckets contained foodstuffs and provisions and were obviously in constant use, but there were also beautifully crafted blue glass vessels and fine bowls from abroad, gifts from allies and neighbouring leaders. Rich hangings shielded some parts of the interior and divisions but it was quite spacious for only two individuals plus a few cattle and goats as now.

The stranger walked directly to the central fire, stretching out his hands to make the best of its friendly warmth. Wulfgar poked about in the flames to make it perk up and the sparks flew when he placed fresh logs on the embers. With that done, he turned about to find a stool for the stranger, which he deposited close to his own by the fire.

'Here, rest your person, Sire. You must have walked far? A horn of mead to drink your health, Sire, and warm the limbs?' He wondered what had come over him to be so polite to a man he did not know. He even offered him one of his favourite gold-rimmed drinking horns.

Again he noticed the raven. It hovered on the stranger's shoulder and seemed to be communicating with him. A raven. A creature of the wild. There were no words, not even a raven's call, yet Wulfgar somehow knew they were conversing.

'That would be most becoming.'

The stranger turned to Wulfgar with his one wisdom-filled eye above that tousled beard. The light of the fire revealed more of his features and with a shock Wulfgar noticed the other eye was missing. His visitor had rested the spear on a nearby beam and Wulfgar noted it was carved with strange angular symbols. Runes. He recognised the writing style, though he himself had never learnt their meaning.

Suddenly realisation. He held his breath. The Rune-bearer? The Lord of the Dead? The ravens … Was this Odin himself? Or an impostor?

He had just reached up to a crossbeam to fetch a jug of mead. It almost spilled, had the stranger not caught his arm in time and steadied him.

As if he read his mind he said, 'You think you know. But you must be wise and contain your knowledge. It's better that way.'

Wulfgar was lost for words again. The wind was still howling, but the animals had settled down.

A charlatan. It had to be a charlatan. Odin would not stoop to beg entry into a house of the likes of him. A storyteller perhaps, or a shaman? Was this a shaman who had invited himself into his home? Yet he asked not for bread or meat, or even a cot for the night. Wulfgar decided to play along with the stranger, though he must be on his guard. Just why did he have these knots in the pit of his stomach? Then he noticed another raven on a beam nearby.

As the stranger drank greedily from the offered cup, Wulfgar recalled the stories he had heard on his father's knee – the stories he had tried to pass on to his children – of Odin, mightiest of the gods. The most cunning. The most wise. In the guise of Grim he sometimes wanders the low lands with his ravens and wolves. He sends out his two ravens every morning to scour the earth for news, which they bring back to him: Huginn the raven of thought and Muninn the retainer of memory.

And Wulfgar remembered how the world came to be. The story of creation the elders had told in his youth – about the world Ash Yggdrasill, the best of all trees, whose branches cover the sky and under it is Asgard, the home of the gods. He certainly knew about Midgard, the troubled world of men, and he had also grown up with the story of Ragnarok, the doom or destiny of the gods: the 'Götterdämmerung'. The treachery of Loki caused the death of

Odin's good and beloved son Balder. And then there was the end, which starts with three long winters without summers. Perhaps the long winters had begun? Would war and discord follow? Wulfgar remembered the old saying:

> Axe-age, sword-age, storm-age, wolf-age, ere the earth is overthrown.
> Sun and Moon will be swallowed up by the wolves that chase them daily across the sky. Stars will fall from the firmament. Earth's bonds will burst, the mountains crumble. The wolf Fenrir will break free. Fenrir's jaws will stretch from heaven to earth. The Midgard snake will rise from the deep and Naglfar, the Ship of the Dead, which is made from the uncut nails of dead men, will break its moorings down in Hel. Odin will lead the last battle with his golden helm and spear, Thor with his hammer and Frey with his sword.
> There will be slaughter. Nature at odds. The sea will invade the land and fires rise all over the world. Everything will be consumed and the earth will sink into the sea.
> But it will not be the end. There will be a new horizon. A new world will rise above the waters, a green and pleasant land where corn grows richly and grass abounds and the earth will be fruitful.

All this Wulfgar knew, but the message had been challenged of late by men who preached a different creed, who cut down the ancient oaks of veneration and proclaimed a new god, one of love and forgiveness, a healer of mankind.

'You are thinking of the new message the men from Erin* preach. Think not of them. You are your father's son: you are a poet, a thinking man of the sword and a warrior.' The stranger entered into Wulfgar's thoughts.

'I am my own man.'

'You are a poet.'

'I was …'

'… and a warrior …'

'I was…'

---

*   Ireland

'And now? Do you not want to gain entry to the feast hall, to Valhalla? Do you want to join Hel in your dotage bed? Does the blood of your ancestors no longer flow through your veins? Your ancestors were valiant men. Have you been in this land so long you have forgotten them?' The stranger spoke slowly, like one who has seen much and knows much. Had he read his mind?

'I am all you said. But I am tired. No longer have I the strength of the young warrior. I long for rest. No longer can I hope to face an enemy with the confidence of youth. My valiant sword hangs by my linden shield still, but just for show. It joins the lyre that is now my means to speak. My sons –'

'Your sons need a father. A strong father. One who leads and sets examples. I fear for Midgard as for Asgard's fate. Will you join the final battle?'

'You say I am a poet. A thinking man. I no longer see the sword as the only means. The plough and …'

'… the cross?' The one-eyed stranger interrupted Wulfgar's flow of words as if he had bitten into a crab apple. He sighed, a deep, fatalistic and all-knowing sigh. Then, nodding towards his ravens, he added, 'Huginn found you, but Muninn brought me here.'

Wulfgar repeated his thoughts. He had sons and daughters who loved this land. Who had a future here. He was struggling now: 'Some say that maybe Balder has returned in the new religion those men from Erin tell. I am through with fighting. I seek only rest.'

'Rest is oblivion,' said Odin, 'Action is life. Are you tired of life? Then come and join us in the Mead Hall. Valhalla does not open for those at rest.'

He turned to his ravens, 'Muninn, remind him of past glories. Refresh his thoughts, Huginn.'

Then he focused his eye directly on the old man by the fire as he spoke, 'Stop this maudlin'. A Saxon cannot hide. You need one more fight. We both are old, you and I, and our power is waning. Put on your armour. Gird up your sword and hug your linden shield. Stand up once more. These are changing times. Twilight is descending. Even memory will die. Fate calls and rules us all …' Then he added somewhat knowingly as an afterthought, 'Huginn told me of your sons.'

When the stranger rose from his seat, he seemed older than before. More stooped. He almost stumbled, as if under great pressure, under the weight of wisdom and knowledge? The battle-hardened, battle-weary man, god of the slain? Perhaps he was? Wulfgar tried to shake the notion out of his head. Odin would not favour the abode of someone as unimportant as he. His sons and daughters were Christians, as his late wife had been. So far he had avoided the change for himself. His forbears had settled in a new land. He, too, had fought and worked hard for a new beginning. Perhaps the message from the peripatetic Irish missionaries of love and tolerance was the new order? Had it weakened him already?

He had fought the indigenous religion of his neighbours; he had fought the Green Man of the Celts and those who hankered after the blue-painted druids. Now the new faith might unite them. Christianity would stop the killing. A new beginning for all? His sons would be safe in the new land with such a religion.

The ravens squawked as they flew to the door, ahead of the stranger.

Wulfgar decided the man was a shaman traveller after all. It's what his head wanted to believe, though his heart said otherwise. This sad old man could not be Wotan or Woden or Grim, nor any of Odin's various names.

The sadness and seriousness of the darkly shrouded figure stirred him all the same, 'Do you not want to stay the night? My sons will be here presently. They are late. My daughters will return with them. Our meals will be prepared. Where are my sons?' He listened for the lusty sound of the hunting horn, but all was silence, bar the wind outside. The milk cow lowed in her enclosure.

'I thank you. But no. Fate calls,' the visitor said ominously. He was about to turn into the wind, holding on to his hat with his free hand, when Wulfgar made one more attempt.

'Your name, stranger. Will you not leave me your name?'

'You know who I am. You know …' With that he turned and walked away. In the blink of an eye he had gone.

Only now, as Wulfgar strained for a last sight of the stranger, did he notice a pair of wolves, their eyes glowing like seacoals. They, too, vanished silently.

'Odin's ravens … Odin's wolves …'

Wulfgar shook with realisation. It was as if shutters fell from his eyes. Now it was his turn to stumble. How could he have been so blind? He had refused to believe. Odin had called and he had not believed. He had not wanted to believe. He had denied the greatest of the gods of his ancestors. He had denied Woden himself.

All the new ideas with which his sons and daughters experimented … perhaps that was why he had been visited?

Dogs barked wildly as they burst from the surrounding forest. A sad procession came into view. Leading the horses was his eldest son. Where was his youngest son? His daughters walked beside the horses, tearing their hair and crying. Servants walked with bowed heads. Wulfgar squinted his eyes against the wind to make sure. There was a body slung over the back of one of the horses. His heart sank – Eadwyn … it was Eadwyn. Why was it Eadwyn? He stumbled towards the sorry cortége.

Eadward, his eldest son, spoke for all: 'Father, we were ambushed. A band of Celts fell on us just as we collected our kin. Eadwyn caught an arrow in his back. He fell. I ordered the men in pursuit, but Eadwyn stopped me. I wanted to fight, but he bade me no. "Leave them," he said, with his dying breath, Father. "Turn the other cheek as the priests tell. It's what Christ would have done. No more blood for blood …" We accepted his wish, Father and the cowards escaped.'

The sisters took the old man's hands and wiped them with their tears.

'Eadwyn,' said the old man through clenched teeth, '… the Celts?'

'Yes, Father. They took the boar we had killed and they laughed …'

'Eadwyn …' the old man again called out the name, only louder in his pain, as if screaming it would bring back life to the son whose lifeless body he now cradled in his arms. 'May your god receive you. You, my beloved and blameless son …'

The eldest son hung his head in shame. 'I am sorry, Father … but my brother's word … I could not pursue …' Then he added, 'His last words were for you, Father. He asked for your blessing ere he died.'

Wulfgar did not scold him, 'You could do no other, Eadward. Not against your brother's last wish. You have chosen the path of the Christians. That is your destiny. Eadwyn has my blessing, as do you …'

Later Eadward put a question to his father, 'Who was the stranger, Father, we saw leave as we returned? He seemed to have with him a pair of ravens and wolves were following nearby?'

'A messenger from the old country,' his father lied. 'Lost on his way. He knew our forebears, though …'

The long house was filled with kin and friends when the priest said the prayers for the dead. The women cried and the men stayed silent until the corpse was delivered to the earth. Then they returned to the feast and the speeches, the praising of the dead, the toast and libations. Paeans were sung, as were the chants from the old country.

At the head of the trestle tables Wulfgar remained silent, stoic and darkly brooding. His life and those of his ancestors rolled like a sequence through his mind. The upheaval of leaving the old country and the fight to establish a new living on this island in the western ocean. The lives it had cost and the hope it had given them. The old gods had come with them and all the sagas and songs of their past. Albion had become Midgard. Should they now be forgotten? Did those who had been here before them not have rights? There were not many left. Would the new religion mean an end to his culture, like it spelled doom for the Celts? Was this perhaps Ragnarok? Was this the end of the old ways and was this why Odin had called on him to raise his broadsword again? Or was it a ghost who had taken his horn of mead? Was there a middle road? Had his wife Riccula been right when she brought the new religion into his family and later instilled the new creed of love into their children?

As he pondered, another, much darker thought crept into his deliberations: Odin's visit at the precise time of Eadwyn's death. Strange how Odin chose the one moment when he was the only occupant in the long house to call … Odin had lost his favourite son too. Was there no room for goodness in this world? Was the death of his own son Odin's doing? Odin the schemer, the devious magician? His eldest son could handle himself in spite of his mother's upbringing. He was wise for his age and would be a successful leader. There were no worries there. But there was a score to settle that no follower of the gods of Asgard could ignore. This was his fight and his alone. No parent should have to bury their child.

When the meeting was well in its cups and when one by one the guests retired, the old warrior poet sat there brooding still. Until at last daylight began to seep into the weeping hall. It was then he stood up and ordered his lyre to be handed to him. All sound died down as he held the instrument and those who had given themselves over to sleep returned to the table.

He plucked the hemp strings and more spoke than sung the words that had fought in his mind:

'I curse thee, Odin, for thy cunning ways.
I, Wulfgar, join thee and thy wicked race.
Let no man say this Saxon shunned his fate
Whene'er I enter by Valhalla's gate.
Of Midgard's sweat and toil I speak disdain.
I cannot just stand by and see my kinfolk slain!
This blessed child, this Balder of my loins,
His mother's light, whose heaven he now joins,
Shall not go unavenged. This very day,
I break no vow, I act the ancient way.
This brood of fiends that so defiled my age
Must perish by a father's sacred rage.
You stay your hands from Thunor's battle rush
'tis I who must avenge the pup and crush
His slayers from this green and pleasant land.
I join thee, Odin, and your iron band.
This nest of vipers that so rent my life
Shall breathe no more, nor suffer further strife
For Wulfgar comes to fight thy fickle dawn,
While such a crime cries out to Midgard's spawn.
Be thee prepared, old Odin, for my seat
Beside thy table and thy jug of mead.'

With that he laid down the lyre and demanded his sword, shield and armour be brought to him, which he applied with help and diligence. Once more a warrior, he bade his sons to have his horse prepared. Then he spoke to them and all of his company:

'You, Eadward, guardian of the wolves' lair.
You are the head now of this household fair.
You are the lord now, your retainers' host.
Behold your sisters, brothers, wealth and beauty boast …
And hold to values, though their form be new.
You and the cross of Christ. I on the war field's dew.'

With the conclusion of his speech he called for and mounted his horse. His daughters wrung their hands and cried freely when they began to understand his plan. Now Eadgyth, always the more demonstrative of the girls, threw herself at the horse and tried to hold on to him, 'No, Father, no more death, please stay here. We have buried our brother and our mother has long been

with God, we do not want to lose our father as well. Think of us, Father, think of the living, your children and grandchildren. Father, please …'

His jaw set, Wulfgar looked down at his daughter with the sad knowledge she could not understand. His voice faltered when he spoke. 'I must, my daughter. This I must.' And he drove on his horse with his heels lest his heart should weaken and his tears be seen. The horse stepped forward and Eadward caught his sister and cradled her. Then the old warrior poet gave his last command:

'Let no one follow on this bitter quest
'Til sun and moon pass by and go to rest.
I will not suffer you to spite your faith,
This job is mine and Odin's and his race.'

It was a sombre and bewildered company who were left standing in the early light when horse and rider disappeared into the forest. The retainers and younger brothers wanted to go in pursuit, but Eadward reprimanded them, 'This is not my father's wish. We shall follow when sun and moon have passed on their solemn tryst.'

His word now counted and it was not until the following morning that the war party set out in the traces of Wulfgar the Chieftain. The dogs soon picked up the scent and as expected they led directly to the ancient Celtic settlement that had been a thorn of animosity ever since their kin had arrived and settled nearby.

The first of the dead were heralded by ravens that only reluctantly deserted their human carrion, slumped by the covered entrance to the walled and ditched enclosure that encompassed the whole village. The gates stood open unguarded and they soon found others, and still more among the collection of hovels that passed for a village. Men lay dead where they had fallen, hacked and bloodied. They'd hardly had time to grab their swords, their bows and their spears.

They had obviously been surprised the morning after a feast. All the paraphernalia was there, the spit and the fire, or rather the now cold embers of an interrupted feast. Bones of wild boar scattered the site where a carved head with bulging eyes, a small slitted mouth and a long wedge-shaped nose marked the centre of the village. Cups lay trampled, horns lay spilt. Barely a bow or a spear remained unbroken.

'Odin's blood, he must have gone down fighting ...!' shouted one of the retainers.

'Where is he now?'

'Did he survive all this?'

Wulfgar was nowhere to be seen.

The party was wary of attack, but none came. It looked as if a wind of destruction had passed through and the village seemed deserted. Wulfgar was not among the dead, yet they stood in awe of what must be his work. The old man of the lyre and the comfortable chair ...?

Eventually a dishevelled woman walked into their midst. Her hair was torn and wild. Her clothing rent and bloodied, barefoot she walked up to the warriors. A fine twisted torque clasped about her neck marked her as at least the wife or mother of a chieftain.

'You have come to finish what your demons started?' Her eyes seemed dead. There were no more tears. 'They are all dead; unwise young men took on the Saxon foe. They are all dead. Have you now come to kill women and children? The last of our race?'

'We have not come for vengeance. We have come for our father. We hold not with slaughter and with strife.'

The woman sagged to her knees.

'They are all dead. Unwise youth and wise with age. A storm passed through of warriors from the nether world. A flight of demons spread destruction. Your father you say? This horde was led by him?'

The woman collapsed and scratched at the earth mumbling, 'This horde was just one man? Go kill us all, we might as well be dead ...'

Eadward could feel the agony in her heart, as great or perhaps greater than his for his brother. The woman stared up to him, unblinking, perhaps mad, 'Why do you not strike me dead? My father is ... and Braeden, my brother, and ...' She could not say the word, the name of her man, perhaps?

Eadward was bereft of speech for long moments while his warriors stood mute about them. When nothing happened, bewildered women and children came out of hiding, scowling, eyes glowing hate and fright in equal measure.

The woman now stood up. 'You have come to gloat at our pain, then? There are few wounded hidden from your swords. Those fiends did not spare many. Do your worst.'

Perhaps she had not heard his previous request, so Eadward repeated his words, 'We have not come for vengeance. We have come for our father. We see your dead, but not the cause of it.' He waited patiently for her answer.

'The demons fled or returned to whence they came. The imps and giants. The trolls and monsters. Our men fought valiantly, though against those demons they were no match. There is just one who took on human form who stayed behind. Just one for us to hate, on which the ravens feed. You've come for him? You want that fiend who slew our pride and kin? You'll find him yonder by the oak. It's where he crawled at last and where he breathed his last …'

They left her and made for the spot she had pointed out, beyond the bounds of the village palisade. They found Wulfgar's seaxe first. As they approached ravens left, squawking loudly. The last bird to leave the barely recognisable figure carried something away with it in its claw. Swift reaction from one of the men brought it down with his arrow and retrieved its trophy. It was an eye.

'Ravens make no division between Saxon and Celt,' commented one of the Christian Saxons. 'Curse them …'

There were so many wounds on Wulfgar's bloodless body it was difficult to separate armour and flesh. How could he have fought with so many cuts? Spearheads were found in him, arrows still stuck among the cuts of blade and sword. An axe had crushed his skull, but still he had crawled to the oak with his last breath.

They found his horse nearby, mauled and lifeless.

It was only what Eadward had expected. Sadly he gave orders to prepare a bier to carry back their hero. They were also to retrieve the horse and return them both to the longhouse for cleansing

and anointing. 'We shall inter his horse close by, lest he needs transport in his new life.'

Then he returned to the stricken village, to the women who had at last begun gathering their dead. He spoke to them, 'Our father is avenged and so is our brother. We have no more quarrel. Our god is a god of peace. We will help you bury your dead.'

The women spat at him and one replied, 'Do not defile the dead by touching with your unclean hands. We who survive this whirl-wind will bury our dead according to our ways. When the task is done and the days of mourning have past we shall leave. There are too many ghosts here now. We join our kin to the west by the ancient stones and where mountains are the guardians of our faith and where no Saxon treads.'

She looked about her like a mad woman and added, 'All this the work of one man? This storm of slaughter? You are mistaken. This was your Odin's doing.'

◇ ◇ ◇

'Can we not bury him like our mother, simply and with dignity, so God can find him pure? Why burden him with things he will not need?' Eadgyth asked Eadward when the funeral had to be arranged and the grave goods decided and collected.

She was overruled: 'We cannot let down the house of Wulfgar. We have a standing in this land and we cannot shirk from what has to be. Our father would it so. He was not of the new faith, at least not in the eyes of the chieftains of this land. His name shall be remembered and his story told by bards beside fires for generations. If he be with Christ his wealth will not bother him.'

It took several days to dig out a chamber at the place of the dead, to reinforce the walls with planks of wood, add a wooden floor and prepare a wooden roof. A four-yard by four-yard room for so great a warrior. A bier was prepared for the chieftain's body and set up in the resting room. The corpse itself, cleansed, patched up and dressed in his best attire, was kept cool in his coffin, enclosed in salt. There were guards and family with him day and night at the sombre wake. He was never alone. Mead and unhopped beer were provided in large quantities, though the best mead was saved for his afterlife.

The children had not realised just how popular their father had been. Chieftains – some might call them kings – arrived with their retainers from neighbouring tribal lands and set up camp for the duration of the proceedings. Many came with gifts that were added to the grave goods being assembled for show in the long house. It became a statement of family wealth and connections. Most stunning were the beautiful blue vases from Gaul, most large the 'Coptic' flagon from the far side of Europe, most personal the gold-rimmed drinking horns.

When the time came a eulogy was spoken by Chief Eadbald from the north-east, who recalled the life of the dead friend, the past and the recent past: 'Our fathers fought together when they tamed these shores and burnt the forest and cleared the land for tilling. We stood side by side to defend their gain. Many a night did we hunt the boar under the moon, killed the marauding wolves and slew or chased away those Celts that came to bar our progress. Wulfgar died a true defender of his land and kin. He could call on the wrath of Odin, the power of Thor and the strength of Frey. His name will live in mead halls across the land as in Valhalla's walls. Wherever Saxon meet will he be remembered.' Now he lauded Eadward and the family for their good sense of providing a funeral worthy of a Saxon and a chief. There were loud murmurs of agreement, even from those who were known to have allowed missionaries into their midst.

Then they lifted up the bier and, with Eadward at the head, fellow chieftains carried their hero to that prepared place in slow procession.

The younger sons, led by Eanfled, carried his folding campaign seat, his standard, his broadsword and his shield. Daughters and retainers followed with bushels of his favourite oysters from the east coast, bowls of mead and tubs with iron bands which held more provisions for the journey.

They brought his favoured gifts from other chieftains and items he had bartered from travelling merchants, the exquisite beautiful glass their mother had brought with her from Kent as a young maiden. There were gaming boards and gaming pieces and dice for his amusement. All the items were placed into the tomb, stood on the floor or hung on the walls for his convenience on his way to Valhalla. Eadgard placed a few gold coins struck by Merovingian moneyers into the dead man's belt pocket, before everyone left the tomb and the covering of the roof planks could begin.

In a widow's absence the eldest daughter stepped forward to sing a dirge. She was well accomplished in the art of the lyre and for this once she was allowed to strum Wulfgar's instrument. She sang of her love for her father and of his love for their mother and his children and the troubles he had taken to secure their place in the new world. When she had finished and the crying had ceased, she stepped down into the grave room and placed the lyre on the floor.

Then the younger sons mounted their horses and, together with ten sons of similar status and birth, rode about the chamber in a wide arc while chanting a dirge: lamenting the dead chief, lauding his earlship, praising his deeds and asserting their love for him. Twelve riders of the future bonding to the past.

Covering the tomb and raising the mound could be left to slaves and helpers. Now the assembled mourners returned to the long house to see Eadward take his father's chair at the head of the tables where a feast had been laid out.

Just before taking his seat, Eadward took Eanfled aside and whispered, 'I know you want to add ours and mother's beliefs and a Christian statement. I have left Cælin in charge. He will allow you one last visit to our father before we close the earth. You still hold the crosses we received at our christening?'

The assembled guests as well as his kin toasted many a round to the new chief. Sighere of the west Saxons spoke praise to the new chief for the worthy tradition of his father's funeral arrangements and the lavish provisions for his afterlife in Valhalla, while Eanfled made her way back to the place of the dead. A small mount already marked the site of her father's horse.

She pleaded with Cælin for one last look at her father, one last favour, one last kiss. The young man was also a Christian and could not refuse a maiden's wish so eloquently expressed, so he removed a few boards, let down the steps and preceding her down, temporarily removed the coffin lid. Then he looked away, so as not to intrude into a daughter's grief. There, out of sight and unbeknown to the chiefs and the retainers, Eanfled brought two small gold crosses out of the folds of her garment and placed them on her father's eyes, so he would find his way to the new god.

EPILOGUE

Odin was many things to many people, and his name varied among the many tribes of northern Europe. But he was well known to wander the earth in disguise with his ravens and his wolves.

We who think we are enlightened, who have all the answers, what do we know? Did Christianity influence the storytellers and the legends, or was it the other way about? Or maybe both? In the legends Odin hung for nine nights and days on the Ash Yggdrasill, wounded by a spear, to gain magic and the runes. For a draught from the Well of Mimir, the Font of Wisdom, he yielded up one eye. For knowledge and understanding he made great sacrifices. He was also God of the Gallows, of War, of the Occult, the Master of the Dead who moved about his world on his eight-legged steed named Sleipnir. Compared to Christ, though, his motives were selfish.

After all our centuries of Christian heritage we celebrate their memory still – the memory of the chief gods of old: Tiw in Old English (Tyr in Old Norse), Odin (Woden, Wotan), Thor (Thunar), Frey and Freya (Frigga) – every week, on Tuesday, Wednesday (in Old English 'Wodnes-daeg'), Thursday and Friday. Woden under his other common name Grim ('Masked One') left his name in Grimsditch and in Grimesworne. Perhaps locally Thor was the wider worshipped of the gods. Thor is remembered in Thundersley (Thunar's lee) and north Essex used to have Thunderlow, an enclave of Hinckford Hundred, which was transferred to Sudbury in Suffolk in 1832–5. Thunderley in the hundred of Uttlesford is now united to Wimbish. We hear Thor's chariot pass overhead in the rumble of thunder whenever he has thrown his lightning hammer Mjölnir.

'Friggen' means 'courting' in low-German vernacular.

If you enjoyed this book, you may also be interested in ...

Essex Ghost Stories

ROBERT HALLMANN

This gripping compilation of haunting tales includes stories of the distraught countryman of Canvey Island forever searching for his horse and cart; the mysterious haunted picture of 'Cunning' Murrell, the last witch doctor in England and strange wartime encounters.

978-0-7524-4848-0

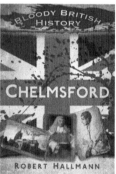

Bloody British History: Chelmsford

ROBERT HALLMANN

From the skeletons lying underneath the city – which include a woolly mammoth – to the executions of thieves, witches, martyrs and murderers at Chelmsford's gaol, this book will change the way you see the town forever.

978-0-7524-8201-9

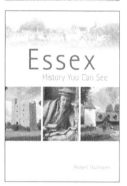

Essex: History You Can See

ROBERT HALLMANN

Including more than 100 photographs, this volume explores the colourful and fascinating history of the county of Essex, focusing on the visible reminders of the county's historic past which so often go unnoticed.

978-0-7524-3971-6

Also from The History Press

Lightning Source UK Ltd.
Milton Keynes UK
UKOW07f0611110115

244290UK00001B/1/P